MW00941150

The Lottery Club

The

Lottery Club

Written by Ilene Thater

Story by Robert A. Farruggia Jr.

~Boo & Ki Publishing ~

Rochester N.Y.

Sue,
Bobby would have
enjoyed you as a
Member of his "Lottery
Club"
Robt A farull
10/14/14

The Lottery Club © 2014 Thater/Farruggia

Boo & Ki Publishing at **www.TheLotteryClub.net**

This is a work of fiction. Names, characters, places and incidences are either the production of the author's imagination or are used fictitiously. Any resemblance to actual persons, living or dead, events, or locals is entirely coincidental.

ISBN: **978-1497389212**

Book design by Thater/Farruggia

Cover design by Thater/Farruggia

Cover Editor Luigino Giorgione

Bobby didn't always know the effect he had on women, but women did. Even when we were young boys, girls would go out of their way for a single moment in Bobby's eyes. He has always had a certain allure that extended to everyone he met, male or female. This may be the one single thing I love and hate most about Bobby.

We met in kindergarten when we were both five years old and already bored with the fact that we were apparently required to show up every day and pretend that the way we formed the letters that made up our names mattered. Apparently, we needed to be taught that the world was a certain way, because the world we were living in did not seem to jive with the things our teacher wanted to teach us. Outside of school we were inseparable. Bobby was the brother I never had, my best friend in the entire world. We shared one of those rare friendships that we knew would extend throughout our lifetimes and beyond. Looking back at those two little boys, it is almost unimaginable to consider the twists and turns that life had in store for them so many years later. It is perhaps the greatest twist of all that inspired me to tell you this story, the story of The Lottery Club.

Chapter One

As far back as I can remember, our families lived in the same suburb of Buffalo and only one mile apart but the disparity in our lifestyles was worlds apart. My dad owned a car dealership, a very large and lucrative business that supported our family's rather affluent lifestyle. Bobby's family lived in a decidedly less classy part of town. Even now I am not sure of what business it was that Bobby's father was in. What I do know is that his name was in the newspaper from time to time and it was always for something that was, in polite terms, borderline illegal. His family always seemed to manage to do okay, but barely. It was in sharp contrast to the life my family enjoyed. The funny thing is, I had everything money could buy and I wanted what Bobby had. Bobby never wanted the things I had. I remember when we were young, after my sister and I had gone to bed, hearing my parents whispering to each other about Bobby's family. At times, my mother seemed overly concerned that I spent so much time with my friend whose father existed on the fringes of 'the mob'. Bobby and I never talked much about his family. It was not important to us at the time. We spent most of our time together outside of school either at my house or riding our bikes and playing in the woods in between our houses. We did, however, spend time talking about my Dad's dealership and how we would both someday grow up and work there. We talked about being business partners. Deep down inside I knew the truth. I would grow up and sell cars. Bobby was destined for much greater things.

I will always remember the first time I saw Bobby. He was in a classroom talking to our new teacher, Miss Violet. She was beautiful and by the end of our first day, everyone in the school knew who Miss Violet was. When I saw Bobby, he was talking to her and in some unbelievable way he seemed even then to be able to charm our twenty-four year old teacher. Miss Violet eventually married our Vice Principal but as ridiculous as it sounds, I almost believe that if Bobby had been a couple years older he may have been able to persuade her to wait for him. All the boys had a crush on her through grade school and Bobby and I still talk about her to this day. She was beautiful and that fact was not lost on five year old Bobby.

Our desks were assigned to us in alphabetical order and as fate would have it; our last names put us side by side in our classroom. Within a few short weeks, we were the best of friends. Outside of school we were almost always together. We played basketball, we played army, we rode our bikes, we built forts and naturally we got into mischief. We were caught one day taking penny candy from the 7-11 store and the clerk that caught us threatened to call our parents. Bobby was able to use his charm to convince her that we had every intention of returning to the store with money to pay for the candy. We never returned with the money and she never called our parents. From then on, she kept a very close eye on us while we were in the store. Regardless of our caper that day, she was always very nice to us anyway.

The summer when we were eight years old, we would ride our bikes to where we were working on building one of the many forts we built when we were kids. This particular fort was an adventure for both us because it seemed like we were so far away from everyone when we were there. Even the bike ride to get there seemed as if it took forever, although a few years later when we were able to drive we laughed about the fact that it was only a mile and a half.

We had just completed the "second story" of the fort one day and we stepped back to admire our work. It was an amazing feat of architecture and engineering for two eight year old boys. We had placed a piece of plywood across a couple lengths of two by fours. We were incredibly impressed with our ingenuity and as we looked down toward the ground we both saw little Shelly Brighthouse smiling up at us. Immediately feeling like our secret fort had been intruded upon by the enemy, Bobby yelled down at her. "What are YOU doing here?" he demanded as she looked up with her soft young face and said "I just wanted to say 'hi'". Bobby looked straight at her, seemingly unamused and said "Hi." He then turned away and we returned to working on our fort as if she had never been there. We continued to work on the fort and when I looked down a few minutes later, to my surprise Shelly was nowhere in sight.

It wasn't until several years later that we thought about that day and realized what an astonishing feat it had been for a six year old girl to walk that distance just to say 'hi' and then turn and walk away. That kind of stuff has never happened to me or anyone else I know for that matter. It happened all the time to Bobby.

The first time I felt bad for a girl that seemed to fall under Bobby's spell was nearly a year later. We had played all day together and Bobby left my house to walk home for dinner just as it started to rain. I watched from the window in my house as a little girl ran down the street trying to catch up with Bobby.

"Bobby!!!" She cried as her tiny sandaled feet splashed through puddles in the cracked sidewalk beneath her. Bobby hesitated, stopped and turned toward the small girl. She was one year his junior and in her rain soaked clothes she looked even younger than her eight years.

"What is it, Penny?" He asked as the rain continued to fall softly from the canopy of trees that covered the street. The calm patience he had with the girl belied the fact that he was already late and anxious to get home for dinner.

"I want to tell you something." She smiled and her dark eyes sparkled as if she had some amazingly important secret she was keeping. Penny pushed up onto her tip-toes and leaned toward Bobby's face, "I love you." She let out a little giggle and quickly kissed his cheek.

"You run like a girl. Now get in your house so I can go home." He said, trying to deflect any expectation the little girl had for the moment.

"But Bobby," she said, "I AM a girl" and the smile fell from Penny's face as she turned and ran away from him. When Penny ran back into our house, I desperately wanted to tease my little sister. As she walked past me toward her room, I saw a tiny tear in her eye and I felt a little less admiration for the effect my best friend had on girls. What happened that day and the way Penny reacted, affected me in a way I can't put into words. I truly believe that it had an effect on Bobby as well.

Penny is my little sister. I am not sure if hers was the first heart he ever broken but it was the first time I remember being really angry with him. I never told him I was upset. It wouldn't have mattered to him anyway. In Bobby's world, whatever you felt was your problem alone... "Get over it."

Years passed. The little girls came and went from Bobby's life. We, of course, continued to be the best of friends as we entered high school. We liked most of the same sports and we both did well in school with minimal effort. Where girls were concerned, it was always the same. I tried twice as hard and Bobby seemed to always do twice as well. No matter what, no matter who... if you were with Bobby you were having the time of your life. Naturally, he was always surrounded by girls. Over the years, even Penny came back around and was hoping for the day he would take notice. There were pretty girls, not-so-pretty girls, skinny girls, heavy girls, girls that were athletic, girls that would look up from a book just to meet his glance. Every girl from the most introverted shy girl to the loud obnoxious air-headed cheerleader was his.

He had his pick. He could have any girl he wanted and Bobby wanted all of them. Girls liked me as well. Girls liked me because they wanted to be near Bobby. So that was cool. I got lots of dates because of our friendship. In high school I sat in a parked car with more than one girl who had stopped, mid-makeout, to ask about Bobby.

Chapter Two

Bobby's first love, as it turns out, was my sister Penny. Her eyes still lit up when she looked at him just as they had when she was eight. That sweet little puppy love she felt for him eight years previously seemed to have grown over time. By the time we were all teenagers she was trying hard to not be obvious around Bobby. Penny tried to act every bit as cool as she could when Bobby was around. It was in sharp contrast to the way she acted around everyone else. Being my little sister, she had been given everything she ever wanted, much more so than I had. She was cute and her personality had grown a tiny bit pretentious for my liking. Bobby didn't seem to mind. They spent every minute they could together. It all happened the summer before our senior year of high school. I could tell they were in love. It made me happy and fearful at the same time. I admit that I was also a little jealous of all the time Penny was able to spend with my best friend. I had mixed emotions about the whole thing and I tried not to think negatively about the situation. Somehow, deep inside, I feared the day I would see my sister's heart broken by Bobby like it had been that rainy day years before. I threatened Bobby. I threatened Penny. It was all an attempt to keep myself from the inevitable pain of seeing the people I loved get hurt.

My feelings didn't deter either of them from seeing each other. Early that summer, they were "officially" boyfriend and girlfriend. It was irritating to me when I would spend Saturdays playing tennis or basketball with my friend only to have the day cut short by Bobby saying, "Hey, I have to go. I need to go home and get ready to pick Penny up tonight."

On those days, I would get back to my house and Penny was there getting ready for their date. She was inevitably in some kind of panic over the fact that something wasn't right. It was always something like her hair didn't look the way it should. Maybe she should wash it and start over again. Sometimes it was her clothes. The clothes she loved and wore all the time were suddenly all wrong to her. It was usually only about five minutes before Bobby would ring the doorbell that things somehow magically settled down and everything was okay again.

It felt funny to watch my best friend take my little sister's hand and walk her to his car. I was conflicted. As Penny's older brother I felt as though I should protect her against guys like Bobby. At the same time as Bobby's best friend, I think I was supposed to trust him. It was weird for me to say the least. I just decided to let whatever was going to happen between them happen. As it turned out, they grew very close.

Bobby liked talking to Penny. Earlier that year, his mom had become very ill. In addition to that, his dad had been remanded to prison a few months prior. Bobby was feeling the weight of the world on his shoulders trying to take care of his family. In some way, Penny was exactly what he needed at the time. He found a way to confide in her on a level he couldn't with me or anyone else. I could see what was happening and one day my friend finally confessed something to me. He and Penny had lost their virginity in the back of Bobby's car one night while they were together. Being the big brother, I desperately wanted to protect my little sister and I again warned Bobby against doing anything to hurt my sister. He explained in great detail how much my sister meant to him and even explained that he had carved their names into the top of the rear view mirror. The fact that Bobby had done this inside a car he loved so much seemed to me to be Bobby's way of saying that he really loved her.

It was only a couple days later that Bobby's mom was admitted to the hospital and never came home. She died the following week. Bobby was devastated emotionally. He didn't want to talk about it, at least not with me. Instead he spent every minute he could with Penny. He somehow managed to let her in and as time passed he started acting more and more like the old Bobby. I finally conceded that Bobby and Penny were good for each other.

I was always afraid that it would be Penny that ended up being hurt. I don't know for sure and I can't explain it with any degree of certainty exactly what happened that fall. To this day, neither one of them will explain exactly what happened between them when they stopped seeing each other. The one event that everyone points to is the day Bobby saw Penny kissing another boy at school. It happened only weeks after we had started the new school year. I know he was hurt and then hurt leads to anger and rage although Bobby never showed it. He did end the connection he had with my sister and even though she claimed it was 'nothing', there was no going back for Bobby. As it happens with so many things in life, the ending always comes long before the wisdom of knowing. I can only offer a guess with the inside knowledge I have of the people that Bobby and Penny were at the time. It was obvious that they loved each other. They were very young and in that one brief summer they were both forced to deal with things that neither of them had the age or experience to handle. Their relationship seemed to mature far beyond their years and neither of them knew what to do with it. I think it pushed them too far. It was too much for two kids to handle.

Regardless of what or how it happened, Penny broke Bobby's heart. I am not sure I realized then, and I could have never predicted, the effect that a broken heart would have on my friend.

At the time, he seemed to bounce back quickly, the girls had never stopped pursuing him and now with my sister out of the picture they were all clamoring to be next in line for Bobby.

One girl in the fourth period history class took the time to find out where Bobby sat in fifth period history. Janie then started writing secret admirer notes for him on the desk. She was shy and different in many ways from the other girls that were always so obvious in their pursuit of Bobby. The notes were simple and to the point. She wrote that she wanted to be with him and then asked the age old question "Do you like me? Yes? or No? Bobby, after reading this please erase everything except your answer." Bobby would just smile and erase the entire note.

Bobby was barely interested enough to find out who was leaving the notes. It took months before he would take the time to show up early for class and see who was sitting at the desk. I honestly believe that for Bobby, the idea of having the girls want him was actually more fun than being with a girl. At the time, he was very involved in sports. He liked girls and he seemed to like the attention even more, but he wasn't completely absorbed by it.

Of all the girls that at one time or another sought to be Bobby's "girlfriend", there was one that never gave up. There was one that seemed to never be embarrassed and never stopped professing her love for Bobby. She was the one constant throughout high school. She was the one girl that could be counted on to make herself appear almost anywhere Bobby went. That girl was Sandy. I was in love with Sandy. She wanted no one else but Bobby. I figured things would probably never work out too well between me and Sandy.

As captain of the track team, Bobby was always early for practice to unlock the equipment locker so that the rest of the team could carry the equipment out onto the field. Sandy was captain of the girls' swim team and she never failed to be at the locker when Bobby arrived.

I never told Bobby that I wanted to be with Sandy. Somehow I have always wanted to believe that in some way Bobby recognized this and that was what kept him from being interested in Sandy. In reality, I think it had more to do with the fact that he was still more interested in his success with whatever sport he was involved in. Girls were easy and sports were a challenge.

One day, Bobby came to me after practice and told me that Sandy had been, as usual, at the equipment locker when he got there after school. She managed to block the door and, once she was alone with Bobby, she took his hand and placed it on her breast. Bobby slowly pulled his hand away. She teased Bobby and asked him if he was scared. Bobby told me that he just laughed and told her that she couldn't scare him with those little things. I was heartbroken that Sandy would do such a thing yet I felt encouraged by the fact that Bobby had not reacted to her advances in the way I might have. As unbelievable as it seems, Sandy ended up being my girlfriend during our senior year. As much as I wanted to be with her, I was never totally comfortable with her after Bobby had told me about the day in the locker. In my mind, I always questioned why she wanted to be with me. In my heart, I always feared that she was with me just to be closer to Bobby. It wasn't until years later and under much different circumstances that they met again and Bobby finally gave in to her advances.

Bobby remained possibly the most popular person throughout high school. He was always the captain of the team in whatever sport he played. He was President of the Honor Society. Bobby won the most prestigious, most sought after award in high school, 'Outstanding Scholar Athlete'. He excelled in everything he did and no matter what happened everything always seemed to work out for Bobby one hundred percent of the time. Things always came so easily for Bobby.

At the same time, my friend somehow seemed cognizant of my life in his shadow. Bobby was captain of the track team while I was captain of the tennis team. He seemed to respect the fact that tennis was 'my' sport and I played first singles on the team. Bobby and I played tennis together whenever we got the chance and he could easily beat me any time he wanted. That actually never happened very often because most of the times we were able to play, we teamed up against the two guys that played first doubles. It was always a lop-sided battle that almost always ended with one of our two opponents congratulating us on the win and asking Bobby why he did not join the tennis team. Bobby usually looked at me, winked, and told them "I don't like tennis."

During our senior year we both applied to the same prestigious college in Pennsylvania. This was the only college Bobby applied to and needless to say, Bobby was not only accepted but he was offered a large athletic scholarship as well. I applied to several colleges and was accepted at most but was wait-listed at Bobby's college. I really wanted to go college with Bobby. My dad was able to pull some strings and managed to pay my way into the same school that Bobby would attend. Everything in school had come so easily to him, winning every scholastic and athletic letter there was to win. There was no doubt in my mind that Bobby would be as successful, if not more so, in college. I was hoping to make it through with a degree in literature with a minor in business with the knowledge I would come home to Buffalo and set myself up in the dealership with my dad after graduation. Bobby was brilliant and chose his career path as a lawyer. It seemed to me like the obvious choice considering his charm and undeniable powers of persuasion. I am certain that some of the situations he had been exposed to earlier in life with regard to his father's business activities may have also had somewhat of a determining factor in his choice, but that is another story. Bobby was convinced that he wanted a career in law. From there he could advance himself greatly in life, perhaps even into politics. I continued to envision a charmed life for Bobby. In fact, life would not be so kind.

Chapter Three

The summer before college was rather wild. Needless to say, I had my pick of any car, new or used, that I wanted to drive off the lot. Even so, I was incredibly jealous of the car that Bobby had managed to charm an elderly woman into 'selling' to him at the beginning of the previous summer. It was a 1973 Dodge Challenger, black on black, and it suited Bobby perfectly. Everyone around knew that was Bobby's car. Apparently, Bobby had seen an ad for a '1973 Dodge Car for sale' and called the number in the ad. An elderly woman answered and Bobby talked with her for about five minutes on the phone.

She agreed to meet him that afternoon. As they were walking out to the barn, Bobby asked her if she had any idea as to the model of the car or its value. She said she really had no idea and really did not even know what it was worth. She went on to tell Bobby that a young man named Andrew from the dealership down the road had come and looked at the car the day before and told her it was worth about $5000. He had offered her $4000. She seemed enamored by Bobby and seemed to want to tell him everything. She explained to Bobby that she did not care for the young man and did not feel that she could trust him. As they walked into the barn, he could see the silhouette of the covered automobile. When he slid the cover from the car, he could not believe what he was looking at. It was a 1973 black Dodge Challenger in showroom condition. His heart leapt at first but when reality sank in he realized there was no possible way he could afford the car. The elderly woman was looking at Bobby and the look on his face must have reminded her of the look on her son's face when he would look at the car. It was love at first sight. She asked him "What do you think of the car?" Bobby said "It is the most beautiful thing I have ever seen," and went on to tell her that there was no way he could afford it. She asked him "Why, what do you think a car like this is worth?" Bobby told her, "I don't know what the guy at the dealership was trying to tell you but this car is worth $12-15,000."

As I continued to wait for what seemed like hours in the car for him to return, Bobby thanked her for letting him see the car and began to walk out of the barn. The older woman said "Bobby, don't you want the car?"

Bobby was puzzled by the question as he answered her, "Of course I do, I just can't afford it. I only have $700."

The woman looked at Bobby with her eyes twinkling and a big smile and said, "I told you on the phone that the money does not matter to me. It is obvious that you will love the car like my son Michael did. I want you to have it."

Bobby wasn't sure he understood at first what the woman was telling him but as she handed him the keys she reached her other hand out to touch Bobby's arm, "Enjoy it and take care of it. Thank you for your honesty. You remind me so much of my Michael. I am happy to do this for you."

I was still waiting in the car when Bobby ran up and got in. He was holding the title and asked me if we could go immediately to the Department of Motor Vehicles office to get plates and insurance for the car. I asked him what kind of car it was and how much he had paid for it. Bobby was obviously extremely excited about the car and I wanted to know everything. He told me that the car had cost him nothing and demanded that we leave immediately to get the car registered. On the way to get his insurance and license plates he told me the incredible story. I may have mentioned this before, things like this only happen to Bobby.

Our social lives flourished that summer and it was the ultimate ending of our 'childhood' and marked the beginning of a new chapter in both our lives. Good and bad.

That summer I worked at my dad's dealership. I was hired to book appointments, unlock cars, clean cars, things like that. My dad had found a way to make it appear as though I was earning my keep. The job also provided me with a way to pay for the expenses I was incurring while keeping up with Bobby. The truth is that the job and the paycheck were nothing short of gifts from my dad. I certainly wasn't doing anything to earn the amount of money I was making. In return, all I really had to do was put up with the good natured teasing I took on a daily basis from the people that actually worked there. I asked my dad if we could hire Bobby to work with me. Obviously this was not a problem, but when I asked Bobby he told me that he could not give up his job working at his Grandmother's deli. He insisted that she really needed him there. We were able to offer him twice the money he was making, but that didn't matter to Bobby. He just wanted to make sure his grandmother was okay. It was the way Bobby was, he never wanted to feel like he 'owed' anything to anyone. I think he felt as though it was charity, and let's face it, it was. He continued to work at the deli all summer. I was again impressed with my friend and his loyalty.

Amazing as it may seem, I often found myself at the deli during my lunch break visiting Bobby. I loved watching him interact with his grandmother, the employees, and the customers. He was working hard and loving every minute of it as he laughed and joked and took in money for the deli hand over fist. Bobby was genuinely happy every minute doing what he was doing. On the other hand, while I felt not entirely miserable about my job, I felt uncomfortable with the knowledge that I was not really earning my keep.

That summer I formed a friendship with the youngest of the salesmen I worked with at my dad's dealership. Andrew, or Drew, as I knew him, was one of our best salesmen and he was just twenty-seven. He was arrogant and cocky, like any good salesman should be. He liked to tell me stories about the wild parties he had at his condo and all the hot women that were always there. One Monday, he came to work excited about a party he was planning for that weekend. Apparently, he had met a gorgeous female singer at a nightclub the weekend before and had approached her and asked her to come to the party. He wanted this party to be particularly impressive and something about the way he was talking made me think he wanted to impress me as well. Feeling I was no threat at eighteen years old, he asked me if I wanted to come to the party. I excitedly accepted his invitation and asked if I could bring Bobby. He thought it was a great idea. He laughed at my suggestion and said it would be an opportunity for us to witness the 'master' in action. He would soon find out it was not such a great idea for Bobby to be there.

Later that day I told Bobby about Drew's invitation and he was not overly enthusiastic about going to the party.

"Drew is a dick!!" Bobby expressed his displeasure at the invitation. He and Drew had met previously and Bobby had been less than impressed at the time. I thought it was because Bobby was jealous of Drew but that was not the case. Bobby has always had a particular knack for reading people. When I explained that Drew had been very nice to me, Bobby correctly explained that Drew was only being nice to me because he thought that I could help him in some way where my dad and the dealership were concerned. I continued to think of Drew as a friend but would eventually find out that Bobby's analysis was right.

I had never known Drew to be nervous or overly excited about anything, but for the entire week before the party he was acting like a love struck schoolboy hoping and praying that Liz would come to the party. He was dreaming that she would fall in love with him and they would live happily ever after.

For the rest of the week I heard Drew making phone calls and making arrangements for the party. Drew had hired a dj and a bartender and was having the food catered. He was going all out and I must admit that I was excited at the thought of attending. If this party was half as exciting as Drew's stories of his previous parties, this was going to be an event. Bobby's attitude about going remained lukewarm.

As we walked toward the door of Drew's condo Friday night, Bobby asked if I was sure that I wanted to do this, or if we should we go out and get a pizza with our friends from school. I somehow convinced him to go inside with me. I was eager to know if all the stories

Drew had told me about the drinking, drugs, and wild women at his parties were true. I rang the doorbell and stood there for a few seconds while I waited for someone to answer. When no one came to the door, Bobby said "C'mon" and swung the door open and we walked in.

The party was rocking! We looked at each other for a moment and smiled. It immediately appeared to me as though all of Drew's stories were indeed true. We were certainly going to find out. We worked our way through the living room eyeing the excitement. There were attractive men and women everywhere. The music was loud, liquor was flowing and a faint smell of pot was in the air. As we walked into the kitchen, Bobby froze. At first, I didn't understand Bobby's reaction but as Liz stepped out from behind Drew, I saw the stunning twenty-five year old singer. It was as though a switch had been flipped and immediately there was a sparkle in his eyes and a light in his soul. Bobby's entire attitude about the evening changed immediately as he looked at the stunningly beautiful woman standing in front of him.

I tried to draw Bobby's attention away from her, but he had completely tuned me out and was fixated on this woman in a way I did not remember ever seeing before. The closest thing I can associate with that moment was the intensity with which Bobby played sports. There was a certain drive, an energy about him that was evident to everyone.

A few seconds later, Drew walked from the kitchen into the next room to talk with the dj and see why the music had suddenly stopped playing. Although he had a dj, I think he wanted to impress upon Liz that he was somehow running the show. As he excused himself from Liz he winked at her and said, "Don't go anywhere, gorgeous, I'll be right back." He was gone too long. Two minutes was all Bobby needed.

Bobby did not wait for Liz to meet his glance before he started walking toward where she was standing. He was only a couple feet away from her when their eyes locked. Bobby did not stop until he was almost uncomfortably close and then leaned his face toward Liz's ear and whispered, "*I know what you are thinking.*"

Liz seemed to be caught off guard for a moment before she finally smiled and said, "And who might you be?" As if he hadn't heard the question, Bobby leaned in again and whispered, "*I can prove it.*" Liz extended her hand and said to Bobby, "My name is Elizabeth. My friends call me Liz." With that, Bobby took her hand in his and as cool as I have ever seen anything portrayed in movies or in real life, he kissed the back of her hand as he kept his eyes locked on hers and simply said, "I know that." He added, "My friends call me Bobby. I will call you Elizabeth because I have no intention of being your friend."

Undeniably, Bobby had Liz's attention at that point. He also had my complete attention as well as the attention of nearly everyone else in the room. Bobby and Liz seemed oblivious to everyone else around them. It was then that Liz looked at Bobby and asked, "So what exactly is it that I am thinking?"

"Exactly?" Bobby repeated. Without giving her time to answer Bobby instructed the stunning singer to think of ANYTHING in the entire universe and to picture it in her head. I could not imagine what Bobby was thinking when he told Liz that he could read her mind and that he could prove it. He asked if she had a piece of paper and a pen. She nodded as she pulled a small notebook and a pen from her purse. He asked her to write down exactly what she was thinking so there would be no question that Bobby knew what she was thinking.

I was dumbfounded trying to imagine how Bobby thought he was going to pull this off. It seemed more than obvious to all of us watching that this effort was doomed to fail. Unless he could really somehow read her mind, Bobby was about to crash and burn in front of a room full of people. I was beginning to feel uncomfortable imagining Bobby's embarrassment when he was unable to prove that he could actually read her mind. Liz had already turned away and was writing something on the paper. "Okay. I am ready if you are," she challenged Bobby as she turned toward waving the small piece of paper folded in her hand.

I looked around the room where I saw somewhere between ten and fifteen spectators, including Drew who had returned and had been watching Bobby's game with the rest of us. Bobby put his hand on Liz's hand that held the paper and closed his eyes. He told Liz to concentrate on whatever it was she had written.

The room had become quiet as everyone stopped talking and waited to hear what Bobby would say next. It was as though they were waiting to hear the punch line of some fantastic joke. I was in such awe of Bobby in that moment that I can still remember exactly what he said, word for word. "Concentrate" he repeated. "I can feel myself moving from this room. I am looking but I do not see it yet. I do not believe it is of this earth. I am floating in space and it is becoming clearer and clearer. It is not any one thing. It is a group of stars. All I can see in the blackness is the Big Dipper."

There were a few chuckles and mumbling between the other guests. I was stunned and in my disbelief I wondered where Bobby was coming up with this stuff. It was possibly the most ridiculous thing I had ever heard Bobby say. Yet he said it with a confidence and a knowing that somehow made us all forget how it sounded and we couldn't wait to see what it was that Liz had written on the paper. Liz unfolded the paper and there were no words or letters written. Liz had drawn the Big Dipper. Her eyes were wide with amazement as her jaw dropped and for a second I was afraid she might faint. Everyone was looking at the piece of paper and the room was full of people standing in shock at what they had witnessed. Bobby just smiled as if to say, "I told you I knew what you were thinking."

While I was still in disbelief at what I had just witnessed, what happened next was almost as surreal. Bobby folded his hand over Liz's hand that still held the paper and said, "Do you want to get out of here?" It had never been intended as a question and Bobby did not wait for an answer before he led her out the door.

I have known Bobby forever and yet I stood there in complete awe of what he had done. I can only imagine the amazement that the other guests that night had felt. In ten minutes Bobby had walked in to the party, managed to find the most attractive and interesting woman there, captured her heart, and then he left with her. Maybe I hadn't truly appreciated whatever quality it was that made all of this possible for him until now.

As Drew stood watching the taillights of the Challenger as it drove away, he looked at me with a surprised look and asked, "Where did Bobby get that car?" I immediately put two and two together and realized that Drew had been the 'Andrew' that had tried to con the old lady out of the car the day before she gave it to Bobby.

I smiled and answered, "Some old lady gave it to him."

Drew was shaking his head and it looked as if he might explode. "I hate that kid."

"That's funny; he speaks so highly of you." I said with a grin.

Under his breath I heard Drew mumble again, "I hate that kid"

Suddenly, reality hit and a rush came over me as I realized that Bobby was my ride. I looked back at Drew, who now looked completely dejected at the loss of any chance he had for his happily ever after with the attractive young woman Bobby had just stolen from under his nose. There was nothing left for either of us but to drink ourselves into a stupor, which is precisely what we did that night. Drew and I spent the rest of the night talking about Bobby and Liz. Bobby spent the night with Elizabeth.

Less than a week later Liz was gone, having left town to go somewhere else to sing. I am still not entirely sure why Bobby wanted to stay in touch with her, but he did for a while. During the week that the band had been in town, Bobby and I had become friends with the rest of the band. He and I even took a road trip a few weeks later to see her and the band in Scranton. That was the last time either of us saw Liz. The letters and phone calls sort of faded away as we started college. I know from talking with Bobby that she would always hold a special place in his heart. I know for sure that from that point on Bobby always had a thing for singers.

I think it was that summer that I began to see Bobby in a different light. He was my best friend, yet I understood so little about his motivations in life. I can only venture my guess as to what it was that made Bobby "Bobby". To some degree, or maybe to a great degree, it was his confidence that made him stand out. When we were both still very small boys Bobby was comfortable with himself. As kids, I remember a time when he told me that he had gone with someone to see a clairvoyant that had told him that he had an 'old soul'. Neither I nor Bobby fully understood or appreciated what that meant at the time. I remember thinking somewhere along the lines of it meaning that Bobby knew things at a young age that only someone much older with a great deal of life experience would have a reason to know. Now that I am older, I grasp the meaning in a much more solid way yet I am still not sure that it explains everything about Bobby. I do know that Bobby had a special talent for being able to read people. He was instantly able to determine the root of their motivations and was able to use that to manipulate them in whatever way he chose.

One thing I know for sure about Bobby is that it's never about winning or losing. That's only because in Bobby's mind, there is no competition. He has already won everything.

Chapter Four

We started college in the fall and we were instantly consumed by our new life on campus. It was almost like nothing else outside of the college existed for us anymore. Bobby was immediately involved in sports and the fraternity rush. Naturally, the college girls swarmed him. I kept myself busy with Bobby's overflow. It was fun trying to juggle classes, assignments and all the girls I was dating. Bobby had no problem settling in to campus life. As always, most of the fraternities and most of the girls were vying for Bobby's attention. Somehow, the coach of the soccer team impressed Bobby enough to convince him to play on the team.

It was during soccer season that Bobby had his longest 'relationship' with a girl since Penny. It lasted nearly two and a half months which was really saying something for Bobby. She was someone he had met not a party, but at his soccer games. She was a scorekeeper for the team and I have always thought she was an unusual match for Bobby. She was definitely not his typical choice. She was certainly not the type of girl I had become accustomed to walking in and finding naked in our dorm room. Most of those girls never bothered to cover up or act embarrassed. I think if I had ever walked in on Dee she would have fainted. Dee came from a family with money. She was cute but I did not really see her as

Bobby's type. I think it may have been her fiery spirit that kept Bobby interested for a while.

Bobby was the star goalie on our team. Soccer was not the most popular sport at our school, but the games against our crosstown rivals at State typically drew a crowd of around one hundred fifty people.

During the games, Bobby always wore two or three bandanas so that when whatever girl he was "dating" that week ran up to him after the game, he would give her one of the bandanas and tell her to wear it to the next game for luck. The night our team played against State was an incredible night for Bobby. It was the second to the last game of the season and at this point he had been dating Dee for only a couple weeks.

The game started out slow as is typical for soccer but since State was a Division 1 powerhouse and we were Division 3, Bobby's goal keeping skills were put to the test that night. Our offense rarely had the ball, in sharp contrast to the other team that was continually shelling Bobby. He was making save after save and it seemed as if the harder they played, the more Bobby thrived on the excitement. I think he made thirty-six or thirty-seven saves that night on his way to a record setting shut out. Every time Bobby made a save the crowd cheered, but there were three screams that were louder and longer than the rest.

As exciting as the game had been, it was nothing compared to what happened after the game. I had been watching the crowd during the game. The three girls I heard screaming the loudest were all wearing bandanas. One of the three was Marie, a nursing student that attended State. The other two were girls that I recognized from our school.

At the end of the game, our team managed to score a goal with only forty-eight seconds left. When the final horn sounded, the crowd rushed the field. Many were specifically looking for Bobby but he had already left the goal and was running toward the locker room at a full sprint. It wasn't because he was scared or embarrassed, and as I pushed to get closer to him I could hear him laughing and screaming, "I never thought all three of them would all show up at the same game for Christ's sake!"

I followed Bobby to the locker room where I found him lying on a bench laughing uncontrollably as he tried to catch his breath. I asked him, "Now what are you going to do?"

He asked me to check outside the locker room to see what was going on. When I finally returned I told him "You are in deep shit, my friend." I then gave him the bad news. Dee, Marie, and the other two girls were all standing outside waiting to confront him. By this time Bobby had all but caught his breath but he was still laughing so hard it was difficult to understand what he was saying.

"I got it covered," Bobby said before begging me to go out and tell the girls he had snuck out the back and they might as well go home.

I did exactly as Bobby had asked and I went home as well. About an hour later he was at our dorm with Dee on his arm. I asked him how he had chosen her and he responded that he hadn't. He explained that Dee had come into the locker room after I had left with the other three bandanas in her hand and what looked like some blonde and brunette hair as well. She had thrown them at Bobby and asked him "What's it gonna be? Them or me?"

Bobby told her that of course it was her, which I believe was a solid choice for him given the fact that the other three had already walked away and weren't really a choice anymore. Dee never brought it up again. They broke up less than two months later right before the holiday break. I always knew that Bobby really did like her. A permanent girlfriend was just not possible for Bobby.

Perhaps the single most dramatic story that really drove home the fact that women would do anything for him is about a girl named Cara. I know without a shred of doubt that Bobby is not a mean or malicious person. Bobby was at times, perhaps, careless. Maybe not even so much with the girl's feelings, but many times with the type of girl he was attracted to. That, combined with the fact that he had an undeniable ability to get what he wanted made for some very serious problems for him from time to time.

Bobby met Cara soon after the spring semester started. Unlike Dee, Cara was his typical girl. She was two years older than Bobby and was in a sorority where the girls told each other everything. Cara had confided that her sisters teased her about "robbing the cradle". It didn't bother her because she knew that they would all jump at the chance to be with someone like Bobby and she recognized the fact that they were more than likely jealous of her. What Bobby did not know is that Cara also told her sisters about how in love she was with Bobby and how they would be married after college. Needless to say, Bobby had no idea she believed this. He certainly had no intention of marrying Cara. Ever.

Bobby, being "Bobby" as I have explained, for whatever misguided reason ended up sleeping with Cara's sorority 'big sister', a girl that had been her mentor and confidant. She had been the one that had relentlessly teased Cara about Bobby being so young, yet she was three years older than Bobby. I can think of no other reason why she would have done it, other than to spite her little sister. My friend was every bit as guilty as she was, but Bobby was just being typically Bobby.

Bobby had never told anyone about what had happened between he and Susie, Cara's big sister, not even me. He assumed that Susie would do the same. Bobby should have known there are no secrets in a sorority house. Needless to say, Cara found out less than a day later.

The next day, Bobby and I were walking past the dorm where the sorority was housed when one of the girls ran out screaming for Bobby to come inside with her. Cara had locked herself in her room and demanded that Bobby talk to her or she was going to jump out her seventh floor window.

We ran in the building and took the elevator up to the seventh floor and as we waited for the elevator I shot Bobby a look as to say, "Now what?" Bobby shrugged and smiled. When we got the seventh floor we could see that Cara really had locked herself in her room. We could hear her crying and when she knew Bobby was there, she started screaming at him through the door asking him, "How could you do this to me?" In between the sobs we all heard her saying how much she loved him and that now that he had betrayed her she had no reason to live.

We all watched as Bobby tried his best to calm Cara down and convince her that if she would just open the door that everything would be okay. After a few tense minutes, Cara calmed down and started talking with

Bobby. When she asked Bobby if he loved her and would marry her someday, Bobby did not lie to her. We all held our breath and listened as Bobby explained that he would always love her but there was no way he would marry her.

Cara immediately became upset and again threatened to end her life. We heard her start to unlock the window in her room and open it. Cara was a small girl and not very strong. The windows in the building were very old and difficult to open. If not for that fact, she may have succeeded in getting herself out the window before Bobby broke down the door to her room. Cara was almost all the way out the window by the time Bobby reached her and grabbed her by the ankles. As I ran into the room Bobby shouted for me to help him pull her back inside. She was hysterical when we pulled her back into the room. After about an hour, everything had settled down and Cara had come to her senses. We thought it was better that we left the dorm. I turned to Bobby in amazement and said, "These women really will do anything for you." I had no idea then the relevance of this statement until nearly twenty years later.

I could literally write a book about Bobby's exploits with the girls at college. There were so many and they all seemed willing to do anything for Bobby. With Bobby and whatever girl he was with at the time, it was never about love, it all came down to the girls' obsession and Bobby's power. I don't believe he ever intended to hurt anyone. With him it was always about the desire and intrigue. He never had any intention of committing to a long term relationship with anyone. The reason doesn't matter, but it seemed as if he always ended up hurting the women that he charmed. He kept a distance from everyone and the moment he felt that a girl was becoming too attached, he would cut and run. Perhaps it was his way of never feeling the hurt again that he felt when Penny broke his heart when were in high school. I think that the relationship he shared with Penny was as much about hormones as it was about real love and emotion. Still it left a scar that never seemed to truly heal. My sister's impact on his life was undeniable.

College was going even better than I had anticipated it would for Bobby. He was making great grades and doing exceptionally well in all the pre-law classes he was taking. It seemed at times that Bobby knew more about law than his teachers did. Bobby's lust for learning the law was evident in the way he devoured every book that was assigned as well as several others on a "recommended reading" list that he had been given. He seemed determined and excited about his future as a lawyer.

Perhaps it had something to do with how powerless he had always felt when his dad was in trouble. I think it frustrated Bobby that he didn't know what to do to fix things. This helpless feeling had an effect on Bobby that is difficult to explain. It was almost as if he thought that becoming a lawyer would protect him and the people closest to him. I don't know and I certainly can't say for sure what was in Bobby's mind. As it turns out, the things he was learning would indeed help Bobby when things in his life started going badly.

It was a beautiful autumn afternoon during our junior year and Bobby had just gotten back a paper he had written for one of his classes. He had done exceptionally well with it, even by Bobby's standards, and he was in an amazingly good mood. I, on the other hand, was enjoying the status quo and had just received a solid "B" on my most recent economics test. We were both ready to party a little bit. Bobby had a soccer game later that day but that did not matter to Bobby. He had already played more games stoned or drunk than he had played sober and it had never affected him adversely in any way. He could flip that switch and God forbid if you were on the other team. Anyway, we had just started to celebrate our individual accomplishments when Campus Safety pulled up. As they got out of their car and started walking it became evident that they were walking toward us. I immediately recognized one of the officers as Keith. Keith was a campus security officer but he had also become somewhat of a friend of ours. Bobby was rather well known for various reasons and at times had been required to use his charm to get himself and others out of a few minor 'situations'. The bottom line is that when Officer Keith showed up, Bobby was ultimately let off with a warning.

As the officers approached us Keith addressed Bobby directly, saying that he needed to speak with him. Bobby was unsure of what Keith had to say but assured him that whatever it was it was okay to say in front of me. It was then that Keith explained to Bobby that the college had received a call and that Bobby's father had been arrested for conspiracy to commit murder. He asked Bobby to please call home right away. Not unexpectedly, Bobby did not waste time calling. He was gone before Keith and the other officer had a chance to say anything more. Bobby went immediately to the campus bank to withdraw everything he could and then sprinted to his car and drove away from the campus.

The drive from college back to Buffalo was a solid four hour drive for most people. Bobby and I had timed our - selves, and kept track of our driving accomplishments every time we had driven to or from the college in Bobby's Dodge Challenger. Our fastest time ever stood at three hours and forty five minutes.

Bobby burst into his family's house in Buffalo just three and a half hours after leaving the college. He was immediately met at the door by his older sister Diana who was crying inconsolably. Bobby hugged her and assured her that he would make everything okay. She could not comprehend the fact that Bobby was already at the house. To her, it seemed like only moments before that she had made the call to the college. In reality had been less than four hours since she had called and requested that Bobby be found and informed of what had happened.

The next words that Bobby's sister, Diana, told him about the situation would certainly put Bobby's resolve and ingenuity to the test. She explained that the bail had been set at $250,000 and although they could use the house as collateral they still needed 10% in cash. That meant they still needed $25,000 in cash immediately. Diana had already spoken with all the family and friends she could and told Bobby that she was able to pull together $14,000. She was upset first and foremost that her father was in jail, but at this point she was more upset with the fact that she had no idea who else she could turn to or what else she could do.

Bobby was now pacing the floor and turned to his sister to assure her that everything would be alright and that he would take care of everything. Bobby left the house that day with what felt like the weight of the entire world on his twenty year old shoulders. He had taken on the daunting task of finding another $11,000 as fast as possible to bail his father out of jail.

I don't know exactly where Bobby went or who he went to talk to, or even what promises were made, but in less than twenty-four hours a very tired Bobby appeared back at the house with another $12,000 in cash. I asked Bobby once where he got the money from and as he turned to me with a look I had never before

seen on his face, Bobby said "Don't ask me that again."
I never did.

A few days later, Bobby was driving an old Chevy
Monte Carlo. It was then that I realized where Bobby
had managed to come up with at least part of the money
he needed for his dad's bail. He had sold his Dodge
Challenger, his one true love. That following week,
Drew began bragging about how he had bought
Bobby's car for $8,000. I started to despise Drew and
his attitude. I understood that it had been Bobby's
decision to sell the car, but the fact that he took
advantage of my best friend in his time of need and
refused to pay a fair price for the car really burned even
me. Drew knew Bobby only sold the car because he was
desperate for the money. He didn't need to be an ass
about it, but he was. I will never know for sure how
Bobby came up with the rest of the money he needed
that day. I was angry enough at Drew, I saw no reason
to look for more answers that would only serve to make
me even more angry over the situation.

Bobby's dad's trial took place over the next two years.
Bobby tried to return to school but he never missed a
court date or a chance to help his dad's attorneys and
eventually Bobby dropped out of college. The evidence
was so overwhelming that in spite of the outstanding
legal team they had hired and Bobby's extensive
knowledge and research abilities, his father was found
guilty.

This was his second felony, which meant that the crime carried a sentence of seven and a half to fifteen years. It seemed to me at the time that Bobby took the verdict extremely personally and felt that he should have been able to do something else, or something more, to help his father. I think it was the fact that he felt that he should have been able to do more that lead to the beginning of the darker moments of Bobby's life.

After moving home from college and after the trial was over, Bobby took a job working in the law library at the University of Buffalo. His amazing research ability made him an asset to the department and within six months he had already memorized the vast majority of information contained in the library. The fact is that Bobby was already a better lawyer than any of those students would ever be, yet he happily assisted everyone that came into the library in every way possible. Again, Bobby seemed to find a way to adapt and find a way to be happy doing what he was doing. I admired that part of his character so much.

Within a year, Bobby became bored with his new job and needed to find another outlet for his energies. Bobby knew EVERYONE on campus. He knew the faculty, the students, the staff... everyone from the Dean on down to the guy that killed weeds that sprouted up in the sidewalk. He knew the good and the bad. Bobby was more aware than most of the unspoken realities that take place on college campuses. Of course I am speaking about drugs.

I can't say why Bobby decided to do it, maybe it was the money but I think it was more about the excitement. Whatever the reason, he became a drug dealer to certain faculty, staff and students that he felt he could trust. Of course, Bobby's character would ultimately dictate that he become the best drug dealer as well. I could see the writing on the wall from the very beginning. This would ultimately be Bobby's downfall.

Bobby was making an extraordinary amount of money. Soon, he had retired the Chevy and was driving a brand new red Ford Mustang GT that he purchased with cash from my dad's dealership. This raised a few eyebrows on campus but no one ever really mentioned it. It is funny to think that Bobby was driving a nicer car than the Dean was driving at the time.

In no way did I approve of Bobby's activities. I had spoken with Bobby on several occasions urging him to stop, but this was Bobby. As was his nature, Bobby wouldn't be told what to do and he would instead make it as clear as he could to me that he had everything under control. "I got it covered," was his only reply. As a result, I felt forced to separate myself from Bobby and his life at this time. It was difficult to do because Bobby would always be my best friend no matter what.

It should have come as no surprise to anyone that over time someone became jealous or someone got careless and eventually the local authorities started piecing things together. They began a comprehensive investigation and it was only days after Bobby had again informed me that he had everything 'covered' that the police were at the college. They arrested him for 'sale of a controlled substance' based solely on a statement made by a student that had been arrested and told the police that Bobby was the person that had sold him the drugs.

The day Bobby was arrested might have been considered a normal day for Bobby. At the time, he was a functioning addict making money hand over fist selling drugs in a college atmosphere. That morning, one of Bobby's regular customers that had been, unbeknownst to Bobby, arrested with drugs came in to buy from Bobby. The customer was a student at the school and had made an agreement with the police at the time of his arrest. He told them he would set Bobby up in return for a lighter sentence for himself. He walked into Bobby's office as he had many times before and asked to buy 8 ounces of coke. He gave Bobby $24,000 in cash and the kid walked out with his cocaine. Thirty minutes later, the same kid returned to Bobby's office and asked if he could buy even more.

Even high on drugs, Bobby seemed to always be on top of his game and he immediately recognized that something was wrong. He asked a few more questions before agreeing to meet the student in the parking lot in fifteen minutes. In his office alone, Bobby took the time to make absolutely sure that there was nothing that could implicate him. He quickly found a student that he knew he could trust and gave him the $24,000 and instructed him to get off campus with it and wait for his call. Bobby left his office and was headed to the parking lot, but the student and two men wearing leather jackets were already walking toward Bobby. As soon as they saw Bobby, one of the men reached inside his jacket. Unexplainably, Bobby also reached with his hand inside his jacket. In an instant, there were easily ten more men standing with guns pointed at Bobby. They threw Bobby on the ground and one was searching him while another one was screaming "Where is the gun? Where is the gun?" There was no gun. Bobby had only reached inside his jacket when he saw the other man reach inside his and not knowing who he was dealing with, he wanted it to at least seem like he did have a gun. It definitely added a little drama to the already outrageous scene taking place on campus that day. When it was all over, Bobby was arrested and taken away.

Perhaps the most shocking news was that just two days after Bobby's arrest, the Dean of the college resigned. In addition to that, two faculty members and seven staff members were terminated. At least fifteen students were expelled. NONE of them testified against Bobby. If anyone had come forward to corroborate the story of the student that had been arrested initially, Bobby would have ended up facing some severe time in prison. I believe it could have been as much as fifteen years to life. That is how deep Bobby was in.

Bobby's saving grace may have been his proficiency with legal matters. He knew better than to keep any written records, drugs or money where they could be found. What it all came down to was the student's word against Bobby's.

After everything settled down, Bobby plea bargained to fourth degree possession of a controlled substance which carried a maximum sentence of one year in jail. Bobby was sentenced to three years of probation and a slap on the wrist. As part of the plea bargain agreement, twenty thousand dollars was returned to the police department. No mention was ever made of the $4000 that was missing.

The immediate result of the arrest was that Bobby was no longer employed by the college. The long term reality was that with a criminal record, Bobby would never become a lawyer. He had used almost all of the money he had made selling drugs to fund his defense of the charges. He had put in a great deal of work on his own case but his lawyer bills were still well over $15,000. In my opinion it was money well spent, but it left Bobby in need of some type of income.

Chapter Five

Bobby started taking jobs doing construction and carpentry work. He earned a decent paycheck doing these jobs, but Bobby was as unhappy as I had ever seen him. He continued to have all the girlfriends he could possibly handle. In fact, he managed to stay with two or three at any given time without actually having to have his own place. Bobby started drinking often and drinking heavily and the consequences become evident almost immediately.

One Saturday morning while I was working at the dealership, Bobby walked into my office. His Mustang was being pulled behind a tow truck. It may be more accurate to say that the car was being dragged behind the tow truck. Although the car looked bad, Bobby looked worse, but I was not at all shocked at what had happened.

It was certainly not difficult for anyone that knew Bobby at the time to imagine exactly what had taken place. As with almost everything, Bobby had pushed his car past its limits. The shiny red mustang that he had purchased only months before was totaled. All four tires had been flattened and the front end destroyed as Bobby slid it across a curb. He had obviously been drunk and I was relieved that my friend had not been seriously hurt and at the same time angry at the thought of what might have been.

Because Bobby had paid cash for the car, the insurance check came directly to him. To my disbelief, Bobby took the nineteen thousand dollars and started his own business. I was proud of my friend for making this decision and secretly hoped he had hit his 'bottom' and was ready to turn a corner to a better life. He was having amazing success with the jobs he had been doing since leaving the college. I was happy, hopeful and excited for him when he used the money to buy a van and tools.

With the start of his own business, Bobby had entered a new phase of his life. The next ten years marked a great deal of changes for Bobby. His business did well. He was the consummate salesman. He could sell anybody on anything. Of course, everyone needed something Bobby could provide and everyone was willing to pay the price. Bobby was undeniably the best at what he did, both in terms of selling himself and the quality of his workmanship. It was almost impossible to tell Bobby "no".

The women still flocked to him. More so than ever, the relationships he had with women were more about what they could do for Bobby than about what Bobby could do for them. Some of the girls provided a place to live. Some provided sex and nothing more. Whatever

Bobby wanted, someone was more than willing to provide.

At the same time, it became apparent that Bobby was slipping further into the clutches of drugs and alcohol. I was more afraid than ever as I witnessed the decisions Bobby was making and the course his life seemed to be taking.

It was almost five years into his business that he met the woman that would become his wife. Her father had money and owned several apartment complexes with his business partner. Her job was to find and hire contractors to work on the buildings. Dana was what I considered a typical choice for Bobby so I was not surprised when he wanted to marry her. I even knew why he wanted to marry her. I had known Bobby long enough to see that he saw it as an opportunity. It might be unfair of me to suggest that it was a marriage of convenience but it certainly didn't hurt Bobby's business when she became his biggest client.

In the days before they were married, there was a virtual avalanche of women coming forward begging Bobby not to marry Dana. There was a girl he had been serious with while he had worked at the college. There was a married woman that Bobby had told he would marry if she left her husband. She came forward to tell him that she was divorced and that she was all his. There was a singer that Bobby had dated that cried as she begged and promised she would do anything if he would agree to not go through with the wedding. It was unbelievable. There were women I had never met before. I was shocked at how many there were. At the same time, I was gaining the maturity to recognize that even though part of me still felt jealous the reality was that the women he was attracting were not the women I would have wanted if they had shown up drunk and naked at my door. They were, as hard as it is to imagine, even more selfish than Bobby was. I continued to distance myself from Bobby's life more and more.

He was married. He was a successful business man and an upstanding citizen.

Bobby was an alcoholic and a drug addict.

He was living two lives and it was consuming Bobby in a way that I would have never thought possible. Although I truly believe that Bobby's wife always knew about the drugs and alcohol, she somehow managed to turn a blind eye to it all. Perhaps it was because he was able to remain productive and for her there were not many consequences. She stayed with him in spite of his addictions. This was in no way the charmed life I had always envisioned for Bobby.

His addiction was eventually revealed when she confronted him one night after he had returned home from work. She was holding a 1099 that he had received that year from a client showing $80,000.00 in income.

Of that, only $40,000.00 had been turned over to the business. The missing $40,000.00 was only the tip of the iceberg. The reality was that Bobby had managed to skim no less than $100,000.00 from his own business that year alone to finance his habits. Bobby was now faced with the fact that his wife and his family knew he was an addict. Not even Bobby could charm his way out of this.

Bobby started making promises. He promised he would quit, but the addiction had carried him so far away that it was impossible for Bobby to quit on will power alone. He spent the next two years struggling with the addiction and failing miserably. It was hard to watch Bobby struggle with something in a way I had never seen him struggle. This was the first time I had ever seen Bobby fail at something in life. It was clear, at least to me, that he was doing it for all the wrong reasons.

One day, completely out of the blue, Bobby walked into the dealership and said he needed to talk with me. He was visibly upset and told me what was happening and that he desperately wanted to stop. I was angry and tired of watching my friend hurting himself. I found the strength inside myself to finally tell my friend things I had wanted to say all along. I had seen him struggling and in and out of the rehabs for too long. I told him that he needed to 'man up' and get into a rehab with the intention of getting better for himself. I told him that it could never work if he did it for his wife, for me, for his family, for his career or for anything else. I still can't believe that I was able to say these things to Bobby and yet that day the words just seemed to flow from me like a river. It was exactly what I had always needed to say and it was exactly what Bobby needed to hear. And that was the exactly the time it was supposed to happen.

I had always admired Bobby. It truly hurt me to see him living his life that way. That was also the day that I told Bobby the sad truth that he had become someone I did not know and that I no longer wanted to hang around with. I was more and more afraid of what would happen next. I want to believe that this had a resounding effect on Bobby. For whatever reason, the fact is that he did exactly what I had told him he needed to do.

Bobby went into a rehab for twenty eight days and on the day he left the facility it was me that he called to come and pick him up. I was happy to hear him say as he got into my car that he wanted to go directly to a meeting of Alcoholics Anonymous. I admit that l had been fearful of what I would see when I went to get my friend, but when I saw Bobby that day there was a light in Bobby that I hadn't seen in fifteen years. Bobby had finally found the strength to surrender and with that he found his ability to overcome the addiction that had been controlling his life.

Bobby continued working very hard in the AA program and eventually realized that he would not be able to maintain his sobriety and remain in the construction business. What was to happen next came as a total shock to me and yet at the same time made complete sense in retrospect considering Bobby's gift.

Bobby called and asked if he could speak with me and my dad. We agreed that we would meet with him, of course. Bobby came to the dealership that same day and we met in my dad's office. Bobby sat down and began to explain that he needed a job where he could count on a steady paycheck and be held accountable. It was obvious to both me and my father that Bobby was expressing a sincere desire to establish some self discipline and structure within his own life. He thought he needed to convince us that he would be the best salesman we had ever had. Knowing Bobby as I did, I already knew that was a fact. My father initially seemed skeptical about hiring him. Somehow, I managed to convince my father that if Bobby said he would do something, he would do it. I knew that if Bobby could harness just ten percent of his ability to charm people that he could be our best salesman and our business would flourish even more.

Less than a year later, Bobby was good to his word and was named "Salesman of the Year". It was only the beginning and Bobby hadn't even begun to hit stride yet. With less than two years sober, Bobby was driven in a way that was reminiscent of the day in college when he was in goal during the game against State. There was nothing that could stop Bobby and he was determined to break every record.

Although Bobby was earning more money selling new cars than our top two salesmen combined, Bobby had a remarkable ability to make a lot of money on used cars. He was the master at the game of 'buy low, sell high'. He was promoted to "Used Car Manager" within the dealership and for another year he was focused solely on proving his abilities and using every opportunity to make more money. It seemed almost fitting that all these years later, Bobby would replace Drew as our used car manager.

As Bobby had advised me so many years ago, the only reason Drew befriended me when I was in high school was to try to advance his career at my dad's dealership. From the day I started working at the dealership after college, Drew's insincere motives became obvious to me. Although he never directly disrespected me I heard it through the grapevine that he would always refer to me as 'the spoiled little daddy's boy'. While I never revel in other people's misery, it was quite satisfying when I had the opportunity to demote Drew to "salesman" status. It was obvious to me that it would not be long before Bobby proved that Drew was no more than a glorified salesman. He did just that. Bobby nearly doubled our used car profits in the first year and never looked back thereafter.

As with all things, Bobby started getting bored when his position became less of a challenge and more of a job. He had car sales down to a science and was easily making in excess of $200,000 a year.

One of the used car reps that frequented our dealership and had sold many cars to Bobby also had a 'thing' for Bobby. It had been obvious since the first time she had come in to meet with Bobby. She was aware that he was married and yet she chased him around making suggestions that in a really weird way reminded me of Sandy in high school.

Katie was in Bobby's office one day after finalizing another deal. Bobby had bought six more used cars for the price of three and as they were signing the paperwork, Katie noticed a lottery ticket on the desk. She tapped her well manicured finger on the ticket. "It is unfortunate for you that I am already holding the winning ticket." She said, smiling at Bobby. "I have known you for more than a year and I had no idea you play the lottery."

Bobby, as cocky as ever, smiled back at the rep and jokingly challenged her by saying "I do play. But if YOU win the lottery, I will leave my wife and run away with you." Katie appeared shocked at his words but seemed to take them one hundred percent seriously. She enthusiastically explained to Bobby that she regularly purchased lottery tickets every Tuesday and Friday night. Bobby said that he would do that as well and suggested to her that whoever won, they would split the money and run away together. Katie pulled a ticket from her purse to match the one Bobby had bought for that night and they both agreed to their plan.

Bobby looked across his desk at Katie and said, "How about a kiss for good luck?"

Katie, overly excited about the chance to finally kiss Bobby, quickly jumped from her chair and leaned over the desk towards Bobby's face. When she was only inches away from his face, Bobby grinned at her and said, "Not me. The ticket."

I am sure she was disappointed but Katie was determined not to show it. Without a hint of hesitation, she carefully picked up each ticket and with an over the top sensuality she kissed each ticket leaving a perfect red print first on his ticket and then on hers. She started to hand his ticket back to him and instead Bobby reached past his ticket and took Katie's from her hand. "You keep mine and I'll keep yours for good luck." She smiled as she said goodbye, thanked Bobby, walked out of his office and out of our building. Our sales rep was absolutely elated.

As the door closed behind her, I stood in the doorway to Bobby's office and said the words I had said almost twenty years before.

"They really will do anything for you, won't they?"

And The Lottery Club was born.

When it was apparent that Katie had gotten to her car and left the lot, Bobby and I shared a good laugh about the whole scene. I saw a look come over Bobby's face and at the same time a thought started clicking in my head as well. We nodded to each other knowing we were on to something. There was no doubt in my mind that Bobby was going to use this revelation to his advantage, I just would have never in my wildest dreams imagined the magnitude and the depth to which Bobby would take The Lottery Club.

Chapter Six

Bobby was truly inspired. He wasted no time in making a list of potential candidates for The Lottery Club. I saw the list as he was making it, before he had made any phone calls. The list consisted of old flames, new flames, as well as girls that might have been considered 'one night stands' if he had actually bothered to stay beyond the required fifteen or twenty minutes. There were a couple I questioned the wisdom of including in his new venture. My concerns were quickly dismissed by an overly confident Bobby and he started inducting females from every corner into his new club. He made phone calls and in one way or another was able to charm every one of them enough to easily persuade them to make the same deal with him that Katie had. I listened as my friend said things like "I have been thinking of you a lot lately…" and "I have wondered what things would be like if we had ended up together…" Once they took the bait, he reeled them in with complete ease. Each and every girl seemed to believe they were special and that Bobby's little lottery idea was something that was exclusive to the two of them.

He explained to each woman that the plan required her complete discretion. He demanded the idea be kept secret and, falling back on his legal knowledge, he required each of them to sign a contract with him. The contract clearly stated that they would each buy one lottery ticket for every Tuesday and Friday drawing. By signing the contract, both Bobby and the woman agreed to either email or text a picture of their purchased ticket to the other prior to the drawing. If this requirement was not met, any winnings from that day would not be split.

I really don't ever remember a time when I had seen Bobby so excited over what seemed to me to be nothing more than a trivial pursuit of a little fun and excitement in his life. It wasn't until I saw the genius behind the plan that I started to appreciate what Bobby was doing. Bobby only needed to buy one ticket for each drawing and then send the same picture to every girl. Although the odds were astronomical at best, Bobby was continually increasing his odds each time he convinced another to play the game with him.

One day at work, Bobby started teasing me and asking if I wanted to join The Lottery Club. I admit that there was a split second when I actually thought "yes" before I came back to my senses. The truth is, he had me convinced and to some degree hopeful at times with the lottery idea. Even I fantasized about a time when Bobby and I would be immensely rich and would travel the world together with no ties or financial restrictions. It is so easy for me to understand the allure the plan had to all those women when I looked at it from that perspective.

I asked Bobby what would happen if HIS ticket was the winning ticket. I wondered what he planned to do when all the women with a picture of his ticket and a contract came forward demanding their half of Bobby's winnings. A huge lottery jackpot divided by the number of women Bobby had included in his game would only leave him with the equivalent of a couple years' earnings at the dealership. Bobby answered my concerns with his usual smile, saying "Relax. Don't you think I have thought of that? I got it covered."

I honestly did not know how he would get around this. I thought about it a lot considering it would have no effect on me nor was it ever likely to be an actual problem for Bobby. I couldn't imagine how he planned to do it, but it was always clear to me when Bobby said he had it covered, he had it covered.

Best case scenario, one lucky lady would win and give Bobby half the money. This is exactly what I believe Bobby hoped for. Once he had his money, he had explained to me, he had absolutely no intention of spending any more time than necessary with the girl. He had no intention whatsoever of spending a lifetime with her. She would be a means to an end for Bobby. It seemed like a very cut-and-dried plan. He confided in me that his only intention where any of the women were concerned was to get half the money. If by some miracle his plan actually worked, he and I would be able to do the things we had dreamed that we would

70

someday do when we were young and hopeful and had imaginations that had no limitations. I assured Bobby that I was more than happy with the life I was living and that all I wanted was for him to find the true happiness that had seemed to elude my best friend. I admit that it was fun to think about the money.

As The Lottery Club, or 'TLC' as we had started calling it, grew over the next few years, Bobby put an elaborate computer program in place to keep track of each of the girls' tickets. It was possible for him to input the numbers and the program would track the winnings each lottery cycle with the simple click of the enter key.

A few months later and completely out of the blue, a girl named Julie that Bobby had sold a car to about a year earlier came into the office looking for Bobby. I explained that Bobby was out on a test drive and she asked me if I knew how much longer it would be before he returned. She seemed agitated and excited but in no way angry. I told her that I wasn't sure when he would be back and with a smirk I teased her by saying "As I recall, Bobby was out with you on a test drive for well over an hour." She smiled back at me and said "That is an absolute   fact. I will be back later." And with that, she was gone.

Because of her demeanor I was curious to know what it was she wanted to talk with Bobby about, but when Bobby returned from the test drive that morning my curiosity about Julie literally took a back seat. Bobby walked inside, high-fived me and said "Another sale, another member of TLC!" He tossed the keys to the lot attendant and in typical Bobby fashion instructed him to "Prep the car for delivery first thing in the morning." Then he winked and added, "You might want to give the back seat a little extra attention." This had become Bobby's way of bragging that he had just had sex in the back seat of the car. I laughed and shook my head as I walked back into my office.

I don't think five minutes had passed before Julie walked back in and asked to speak with Bobby privately. My curiosity was piqued and was definitely getting the better of me. I needed to know what was going on with Julie. I could not hear what was being said in his office, but I could see through the glass walls of the office. I watched as she pulled an envelope from her purse and hand it to Bobby with a smile. Bobby took the envelope from her then leaned over and said something to her before giving her a kiss on the cheek. With that, he walked her to the door in his typical gentlemanly manner and she was gone.

As she walked past me it appeared to me as though her mood had changed from her earlier visit to the dealership that day. She now seemed extremely content and pleased with herself. I watched her walk to her car and as she unlocked the door and got inside I ran to Bobby's office to ask what had happened. I wanted to know what it was that she had handed to him and what it was that he said that had put such a smile on her face. Bobby picked the envelope up from his desk and threw it to me like a brick. I opened the envelope and inside was $17,800 in cash. The money, he explained, was his half of Julie's share of a $65,000.00 lottery win 'after taxes'.

As excited as I was for him about the money, I still needed to know. "What did you say to her?" I asked and Bobby was more than willing to tell me what I needed to know.

"I said 'Very nice darling. Next week it will be my turn to call you to tell you that we hit the jackpot and to get ready because I am coming to pick you up.'" Then he laughed and added, "It's probably not going to happen, but it keeps them coming back!"

I admit that I was a little shocked that Bobby had just been handed almost $18,000 in cash and was acting as casual as could be about it. I asked Bobby if this was the first time it had happened.

"You've got to be shittin' me." Bobby said as he laughed and invited me over to his side of the desk. I was looking at his computer screen waiting for him to open the TLC file when I noticed that the date on his computer was one day off. I pointed out to Bobby that it was the 11th of November, not the 12th of November as the calendar on his computer clearly showed.

"I know," Bobby said, "I like it that way. I don't want it fixed." The fact was, and I completely understood why, Bobby did not want some IT guy messing around with his computer that held his precious lottery club program and files.

Bobby typed in his nine digit security code to open the program. I was as shocked at the fact that he trusted me with his security code as I was at what I saw come up on Bobby's screen. The security code brought me back to that summer before college. For a moment I reminisced about the fun we had that summer. The nine-digit code was *bigdipper*. I instantly recalled that feeling of disbelief I had that night when Bobby seemed to read (as he called her) Elizabeth's 'mind'. That feeling quickly paled to what I felt when Bobby's elaborate program for tracking The Lottery Club was revealed to me. He walked me through everything his program could do. It tracked, individually and week to week, each of the girls' numbers. With a click of his mouse he could track exactly which girl had won and how much she had won each week. The only thing Bobby had to do was enter the winning numbers and the program would scan through all the tickets for that lottery and instantly calculated what Bobby's half would be 'after taxes'.

He clicked on another icon and a spreadsheet detailing the lottery from the day before appeared. The spreadsheet showed a total amount of winnings for the day at $17,843. I commented that it was a damn good program even though it was off by $43. With yet another click Bobby corrected me by showing where two other girls had won. One had won $80 and one had won $6 making Bobby's share exactly $43.

He laughed and said, "I am still waiting for them to report in."

At that point I had to know how much he had won since the day this had all started a little more than two years before. Bobby stared directly at me, waiting for my reaction as he clicked again and the information I wanted to know was right in front of me. Ninety two thousand six hundred forty four dollars. After taxes. And that includes the $28 my tickets have paid out in the past two years." Bobby added with a smile. He then told me about the time his ticket had won $21 with his numbers and it ended up costing him $1,176 after he paid each of the girls their 'share'. When all was said and done, Bobby had basically averaged a little more than $45,000 a year with his little club. Interestingly enough, it was about the same amount of money some of my salesmen were making.

"What are you doing with all the money?" I asked.

In a much nicer tone than he had used years earlier, his response was "Don't ask me that again." I hesitated for a moment thinking I had overstepped my bounds, but Bobby laughed and broke the tension I was feeling by saying, "I am saving it for a rainy day."

That day in front of his computer I also noticed that, if I had read it correctly, there were 68 members in Bobby's club. I knew that I could get back on the computer anytime I wanted and with the password could learn anything I wanted to know. I also knew myself enough to know that I could never break the trust between us. Anyway, I had a feeling that Bobby had installed some type of counter or a record of log-ins somewhere that would let Bobby know if someone else was looking at his program. Knowing Bobby as I did, I was willing to bet on it. I also knew that my friend would tell me anything I wanted to know, which made snooping around behind his back completely unnecessary. It felt good to know that Bobby trusted me like that, it felt genuine and I knew he wasn't playing me like he was playing the girls.

Chapter Seven

Over the next few years, Bobby added even more girls. There were only a few that are even worth mentioning. One, amazingly, was his housekeeper. Bobby had not had sex with every girl, but it is fair to say that he had been with the vast majority of them. His housekeeper was no exception. I feared that Bobby had crossed a line and even I could see that she had feelings for Bobby. It seemed like the potential was there for the game to become far too personal for her and it would lead to problems with his wife. Bobby casually dismissed my concerns with a laugh and his assurance that there was nothing to worry about.

I had concerns about another woman that joined TLC a few years in. Being someone that Bobby and I had both known in high school, I am unsure as to whether my concerns had any basis in fact or if they were a product of both my own personal fears and my pride. Sandy became one of the women in Bobby's club and the truth is that I never knew quite what to think about it since Sandy had been my girl during our senior year.

One rainy Saturday afternoon, I had gotten back from lunch and was on my way back to my office. As I passed Bobby's door, Bobby saw me walking by and I acknowledged him without saying anything as I noticed that he had a couple that looked to be about our age with three little kids in his office. Bobby immediately called me into the office as he said, excitedly, "Denny, look who is here!"

As I walked into the office the woman turned to face me and it took only a minute and then I realized it was Sandy. She was still an attractive woman, but it was clear that the years and the children had taken a toll on her body. Her slender young swimmer's body had grown into a more curvy woman as one might expect of a forty plus year old woman with three children. Bobby introduced me to her husband and the kids and explained that they were purchasing a brand new minivan. All the necessary papers had been signed and they had made arrangements to take delivery of the car two days later.

We all exchanged pleasantries as we shared details of our lives, very obviously glossing over details as we each struggled to convince ourselves and each other that our lives had turned out perfectly. We laughed a little about high school until her husband seemed to zone out and the kids became impatient without something to do. I told Sandy's husband that it had been a pleasure to meet him and I leaned toward Sandy with a quick kiss on her cheek as I told her how good it had been to see her again.

Sandy and her husband returned two days later to take the car home. A week later, Sandy showed up without her entourage asking for Bobby to show her some things on the new car. Bobby quickly agreed and left with Sandy. Almost two hours had passed when Bobby walked back inside with a smirk and the thought came effortlessly into my head as if I knew without even asking.

"You did, didn't you?" I said as he started laughing.

"I'm not sure that I know what you are asking." He said as if taunting me to actually say the words.

"You know what I mean," I said "Is she a member of The Lottery Club?"

I knew Bobby would not lie to me, but the truth is that I already knew his answer.

"Of course she is." Bobby answered.

"And??" I asked.

"Of course."

I admit that I felt instantly betrayed. I can't even say why. It had been more than twenty years since I had been with Sandy. We broke up in high school. I had reached a point long ago where I didn't want her anymore. I hadn't even thought about her before the day she had come to the dealership to buy a car. I certainly didn't want her now, but somehow I felt like Bobby had taken something away from me. In reality, he could never really take something that had never really belonged to me and would clearly never really belong to Bobby either. Still, I felt the sting. After all those years, what I had once felt for Sandy was apparently no longer sacred in Bobby's eyes. He had finally taken her from me.

I was still wrapped up in my own thoughts about the situation when I heard Bobby say "You don't mind, do you?"

It was obvious to me that he didn't really care how I felt about what he did with Sandy. He certainly didn't care what my answer would be. I felt a rush of anger that I quickly squelched as I replied, very snidely, "What's the difference anyway. You can't un-fuc… I mean you can't un-ring a bell, can you?"

Bobby seemed to understand that he may have overstepped but in true Bobby fashion it was, as always, my problem and not his.

"Good point." He said in an effort to put an end to our conversation.

He went into his office as I pondered the fact that I could at least find some solace in the fact that Sandy was the first girl that I'd had before Bobby did. I knew I had to let it go. I was smart enough to realize it had meant nothing even if it did put the tiniest dent in my ego.

Perhaps the single most interesting person that Bobby met during that time was Elaine. She was unlike the other woman that came to see Bobby, yet it was he that she was drawn to the moment she walked in. As I enviously watched my friend escort yet another beautiful woman into his office my mind played out the course of events that were about to transpire. This had happened so many times that it was almost too easy to predict by now how things would go. He would make sure that she knew that he was everything she needed. She would feel like there was something special happening. Her heart would race and she would think this was 'the' moment, unlike any other. But she would be wrong. Lisa had left his office two hours earlier with a racing heart and a brand new car. She had been the newest member of the club up until the moment Elaine walked in.

I watched what I could see through the glass walls without being obvious. To me it seemed as though things were going according to Bobby's plan. Then as soon as that thought hit me, her face turned slowly away from Bobby and toward something outside that had caught her attention. I saw the teardrop run down her face and roll off her cheek. I looked away quickly, afraid that she might see me from the corner of her eye.

I suddenly felt as though I shouldn't be watching. I pulled paperwork from a drawer and started working on running my own business. There had been times when it was hard to remember whether I was coming to work at my dad's dealership or coming to work at Bobby's lottery club. This was decidedly not one of those moments. I didn't even know her, but I needed to know what had happened to make her cry in Bobby's office. And as a guy, I wanted to know how to fix it so she would stop. That one single tear I saw was making me inexplicably uncomfortable.

She left the dealership after an hour and a half with Bobby. She left without buying a car. She left without the excitement and the drama that we had come to expect.

"What was that all about?" I demanded as I stood with Bobby inside the door to the dealership as he returned from walking Elaine to her car.

Bobby calmly told me that she would be back. A friend of hers had referred her to the dealership and he assured me that the sale was a done deal. Then he added, "Six weeks ago she was in a car accident with her fiancé. He was killed instantly. She needs a new car and I am going to sell her whatever car she wants."

So that's what it was. That one quality made a world of difference. She was wounded and in spite of the fact that it appeared, at least to us that the physical wounds had healed, the emotional wounds were still extremely raw. She didn't stand a chance against Bobby and I immediately felt a need to warn him. I didn't know why

I felt the need to protect Elaine since I had never been concerned with the other women. What he would do when she came back in again wasn't fair. I was certain she would be buying lottery tickets before the week was over. I couldn't stop thinking of her face and the tiny tear that had fallen. She was, in my opinion at least, perhaps the most genuinely real woman that had ever graced our dealership and that made her more beautiful. It is true that I felt some kind of sympathy for her. It is also true that I felt jealous that it had to be Bobby, again. I had heard him tell her as he walked her out to the car she had borrowed that she could call him anytime she wanted and that he would always make the time to talk with her.

She was back at the dealership three days later. I brought her into my office as I introduced myself again and invited her to sit down with me. We talked while we waited for Bobby to return from a test drive. I found myself locked on every word she said and at the same time totally lost in her beauty that in no way could ever overshadow her quiet confidence and her courage. In ten short minutes I felt like I had known her forever.

When Bobby returned, they went into his office before going out onto the lot and after a few unusually short test drives they were back inside filling out contracts. She bought exactly the car that I would have selected for her. It suited her and I was happy for her. She came back in the next day to pay for the car. I feared I would never see her again and at the same time I feared she had been caught in Bobby's web.

I started seeing her again only days after she purchased the car. She went into Bobby's office where they talked and then she left. This went on for a few weeks and I started noticing that this was different. He was still his normal confident self but he seemed more genuine with her than I was used to seeing. When I asked about it, I was given the answer, "She is a friend."

She was routinely stopping in to see Bobby a couple times each week. Sometimes she would get there while Bobby was busy with someone else. She was always willing to wait. If I wasn't busy I would bring her into my office. Our conversations were always very light. I know it was nothing like the conversations she had with Bobby. I was willing to take whatever I could get. I envied Bobby's relationship with her.

I remember one time in my office while she was waiting for Bobby; she asked if she could ask a personal question. I was instantly excited and hopeful at the fact that she seemed interested in knowing something personal about me. With every effort to be as seductive as Bobby had ever been, I flirtatiously told her, "YOU can ask me anything."

To my utter dismay, she continued without the slightest acknowledgement of my advances, "Who is the pretty girl on the poster in Bobby's office?"

I gathered my thoughts as the conversation shifted again back to Bobby and happily explained that the woman on the poster was Bobby's wife, Dana. "Dana is extremely allergic to all nuts." I said with a giggle. She had become very active in spreading awareness of the allergy and had become the 'poster child' for nut allergy awareness for the upstate New York area.

I had secretly hoped that by pointing out that the woman in the poster was Bobby's wife, it would accentuate the fact that Bobby was a married man. Perhaps it was an effort by me to make me seem more eligible by making Bobby off limits.

Just then, Bobby poked his head in to say "Hi" and off the two of them went.

It struck me that their relationship in ways mirrored the relationship he had with Penny when we were teenagers. Penny had been there for him when his mom had died. They had shared an extraordinary friendship back then and he seemed to be doing for Elaine what my sister had done for him all those years ago. I was happy that she had someone she felt comfortable talking with. I wished more than anything that it could have been me.

A few months later I found an opportunity to talk with Bobby about Elaine. I asked the obvious question and was surprised by his answer. I was shocked to hear Bobby say that he was not 'sleeping' with Elaine. I wondered to myself whether or not it could be possible to have a relationship with her. I didn't wonder for long. I was single and she was single. I asked her to dinner and she accepted. I took her to a place I knew she would love. The next day we were together again. We started going places and doing things together as much as possible. She was an amazing human being, the kind that was as happy to dress up and go to a nice restaurant as she was to order a pizza and lie outside on a blanket and eat as we looked at the stars in the clear summer sky. We became close friends as well, although in the beginning we never talked about Bobby and we never really talked about the accident. I knew she had fallen for Bobby. I also knew how smart she was and she knew that Bobby would be forever off limits to her. Maybe I was again the consolation prize, but when I was with her that didn't seem to matter. Whatever it was that had lined up in the universe for her to be sitting there next to me, that was good enough for me.

It seemed as though we never really discussed my past history. Only one time did I ever talk with her about my ex-wife's indiscretions. I told her that I had been divorced after finding out that my wife was having an affair. The affair had been going on for nearly two years when I found out. Elaine smirked and said "Don't tell me that she was cheating on you with Bobby!"

"Knowing Bobby that would not have been out of the question, but what actually happened was worse. She was having an affair with one of the women she worked with. I never knew it, nor would I have ever imagined it possible until I saw it with my own eyes… in my own bedroom. That was the end."

I had at times wondered myself it would have been better or worse to find her with Bobby. I had since decided I could no longer afford the luxury of my indulgence in thoughts that made me feel both sad and angry. I had long ago decided I needed to let it go. I didn't want to talk about it, but I knew that Elaine was interested and I wanted more than anything for her to feel that she could truly ask me anything and know in her heart that she would get an honest answer. I felt closer to her for having let her in and in some strange way, the wound healed again in the moment she smiled and changed the subject.

The subject was never mentioned again. I think that by letting my walls down a little bit, she too let her guard down and became more comfortable with me.

Eventually she started talking about what had happened with her fiancé. She cried a lot and I did everything I could to make her feel better. The first time she wanted to spend the night with me, I couldn't help but feel as though I had finally taken something from Bobby. Somehow, it was a shallow victory considering what had just happened with Sandy. Either way, that really didn't matter. What mattered was that I had a part of her, she was with me. I would have done anything for Elaine.

As time went on, their friendship continued as my feelings for her grew more and more hopeless. It hurt to see her come in to see Bobby. It hurt to see her trying to discretely text him when she was with me. There were times I wanted to end it. I was afraid she was going to break my heart, but I was letting her break my heart every time I saw her smile at Bobby like she never smiled at me. There was no way I could let her go. I loved her. To quote Bob Marley, 'Everyone is going to hurt you. You just got to find the ones worth suffering for.' To me, she was worth it.

One day I heard her voice texting and I was certain I had heard her say the word 'lottery'. My heart sank as I started to believe that Bobby was going to win again. When I had asked her only weeks before, Elaine had insisted that she would never play the lottery. He words were, "The universe is much too cruel to me. I will never win, so I don't play." I asked her again about the lottery after I had heard the text and all she would say to me then was, "Don't ask… Please." I did not ask again.

Chapter Eight

Lori was an early member of the club and had been one of Bobby's singer 'friends'. She was extremely strong willed and I remember advising Bobby against including her. The day that Bobby broke up with her she had acted very much like Cara had when she tried to jump out the window in college. Lori had actually lay down on the pavement of the parking lot in front of Bobby's car and kept him from pulling out of the parking spot. Each time Bobby tried to jockey around her she would move closer to the tires. I had the unfortunate experience of witnessing this disaster because Bobby had been afraid of something like this happening and wanted me along as a witness. We both knew she was capable of doing something crazy and she certainly didn't disappoint us. After a couple times, Bobby got tired of trying to drag her far enough away from the car so he could jump back into the car and put it in gear fast enough to get away.

"This bitch is just too crazy and too fast. Hold on." Bobby said as he put the car in reverse and throttled it across the apartment complex lawn and into the next parking lot where we were able to make our escape.

Years later, she had been one of the girls that called and asked Bobby not to get married. I knew that she had managed to keep the flame alive and I saw her as a potential problem.

She stormed into the dealership one day demanding to see Bobby. As luck would have it, he was alone in his office where no one but me was privy to the drama. She informed him in no uncertain terms that she was "sick and tired of waiting" for one of them to win the lottery. She was "broke, unemployed, and sick of everything" and she had no qualms about sharing everything with Bobby's wife. She was clearly an emotional mess and was holding the very contract that she was threatening to show to Bobby's wife. Bobby calmly took her into his office and closed the door. I continued to watch as Bobby worked at defusing the situation. In no way could I hear what was being said in the other side of the closed door, but Bobby was holding her in his arms. She handed Bobby something and he dropped it in his shredder and opened a drawer in his filing cabinet and pulled out an envelope and handed it to her. He gave her a kiss on the cheek, she gave him a kiss on the lips, and they both walked out of Bobby's office.

I never saw Lori after that day. I had assumed that day that they had mutually agreed to destroy the contract, but I still wondered what had been in the envelope he gave her. I asked and Bobby told me. With his usual wink, Bobby said "I gave her a little something for a rainy day."

In the end, there were probably two or three girls that dropped out due to their lack of interest. Another two years later, Bobby's Lottery Club had netted him in excess of $250,000 and there were more than a hundred members.

As exciting as this story is to tell it pales to the excitement, the tragedy, and the twists and turns that were yet to ensue when one of The Lottery Club members actually won the lottery jackpot.

A few days before that was to happen, we were scheduled to participate in the all-city tennis tournament. Bobby and I had continued to play together since high school and, of course, Bobby won our age division in the tournament easily every year. In the years since high school we had always found the time to play together at least once a week. Although it continued to be Bobby that would consistently win, there were rare occasions when I was victorious. I like to think it was because I, too, was a phenomenal tennis player and not because Bobby was doing me a favor. I am not sure I will ever know the answer to that. More accurately, I am not exactly sure I would want to know the answer to that. The fact was that Bobby was extraordinarily talented at anything he found a passion for. However, that year with his obsession with The Lottery Club, Bobby had somehow managed to isolate himself from everything else that was going on. In spite of the fact that I had challenged him to practice with me on several occasions, Bobby wasn't interested. In the end, it was a couple of my other tennis friends and Elaine that kept me in form. I think Bobby and I may have played, at the most, two or three times. Bobby was again the defending champion and I was finding it harder and harder to believe that he would even show up. One day after he had again refused my offer of a workout and tennis practice together, I asked Bobby about defending his title in the forty-plus age bracket. I was informed in no uncertain terms that he was not at all interested in playing this year. Knowing how unlike Bobby it was to rise to a challenge, I continued to press him about it. After about a week, my persistence as well as my insistence finally paid off and I had my friend excited and looking forward to the competition again.

I was certainly not intimidated by his participation. The truth is that in all the years we had both played in the tournament I had never actually played against Bobby. The explanation of that is quite simple. Bobby was seeded so much higher than I was that he never really had to play in the first two or three rounds. I had traditionally been eliminated by the time Bobby needed to pick up his racquet and play. On the rare instances when I did manage to make it through the qualifiers, I was always matched against a very strong opponent. The matches were typically very close, but I never made it to the quarter-finals.

I was determined that this year would be different for me. I was inspired by Elaine's devotion and her belief in me. I was so in love with her and I knew she would be there watching me. I wanted more than anything to put on a good show for her. I wanted to prove to her that I was capable of winning. Moreover, I needed to prove it to myself. Deep down inside I wanted to play against Bobby. I wanted to win. Elaine was my girlfriend, but at the same time I doubted myself and feared the relationship she and Bobby shared. I needed to win and more importantly I needed to beat Bobby.

The first day of the tournament I was as ready as I could have ever been. I felt confident. The first two rounds were a breeze. While Elaine watched I swept both opponents in three sets. I could hear Elaine cheering for me and suddenly I was back in high school, only I was better. I felt invincible.

Bobby was never there to watch me play but I made a point to be there while he was on the court. His first match had been a barn burner and I don't think I had ever seen Bobby struggle the way he was struggling that day.

As I watched Bobby's matches, I again recalled the game in college against State. Today, as had happened that day, Bobby had more than one woman in the stands cheering for him. This time it wasn't college co-eds but an assortment of members of Bobby's lottery club. The women seemed to come and go throughout Bobby's matches. I did notice, however, that it was Katie that had been there from the beginning right through to the end every time Bobby stepped onto the tennis court.

I would have never anticipated how the tournament would play out, but the fact is that truth is stranger than fiction.

On the final day, in the final match it came down to me against Bobby. I was playing possibly the best tennis of my life and had made it all the way through to the finals. While it is true that I had wished for a time when I could play against Bobby at this level, never did I imagine what it would actually be like to see Bobby on the other side of the net from me. My fear was quickly overshadowed by the disbelief I felt that it was really happening. I suddenly felt excited again at the thought of how my greatest fear was setting up to be my greatest conquest.

As the match played out we were tied at two sets each and I had beaten Bobby handily in the last set. I felt incredibly strong and I truly believed that I would be victorious. The crowd had been unusually quiet from the moment Bobby served the first ball. Perhaps they were in disbelief at what they were witnessing. Many of these people knew both Bobby and I. The people that watched knew that Bobby had been the winner every year as we had moved from age bracket to age bracket. It was also common knowledge that Bobby and I were best friends. It felt as if they all knew what I was feeling, that this was much more than just another game of tennis. I won the first game and as I looked over at Bobby he seemed totally disinterested. It appeared as though he really did not care to be there and I wanted so badly to believe that he was not 'letting' me win. I wanted to believe I was beating him because I was a better player than he.

I served a rocket past Bobby and he never even got a racquet on it. It was the first time I had aced him in the match and all I could hear was Elaine cheering for me.

"Get 'em, Denny! You can do it!"

The very second her words hit my ears I instantly thought to myself 'oh no, please shut up' because I knew with every ounce of my being what would happen next. I was right.

I looked at Bobby and knew that he had heard Elaine loud and clear. I saw the switch flip in Bobby's eyes and he immediately looked ten years younger. He had his focus back and, needless to say, I didn't win another game from him and it seemed as if I could barely win a point for that matter. Elaine had stopped cheering. Now it was Katie's voice that was heard so clearly over the crowd. The two women were sitting only two seats apart and I am certain that Elaine had noticed Katie even though Katie did not seem to notice Elaine.

When the smoke finally cleared, it was Bobby that emerged victorious that day. I suppose that made everything okay with the universe again.

We walked to the locker rooms where we both showered before leaving but no words were spoken. Bobby told me nothing of his plans for the rest of the day, but he had apparently told Katie to meet him back at the dealership for what would obviously be some type of sexual encounter as a way of both celebrating his victory and rewarding her for her support.

Elaine and I had instead opted to go for a quick bite to eat together. I also needed to stop by the office to see if an important fax that I had been waiting for had come in while we had been at the tournament. When we got to the dealership I saw both Katie's car and Bobby's car parked side by side. Under other circumstances I would have driven away knowing what was going on inside. Instead, I saw an opportunity. I told myself, and Elaine, that I really needed to see that fax. In reality, I wanted to interrupt Bobby and at the same time I could expose Elaine to what it was really like in Bobby's world. I needed her to know exactly what was going on inside. I wanted to somehow make myself feel safe with her. I thought if I could expose her to this, it might deter her-even if only slightly- from the feelings I somehow felt she had developed for Bobby.

We walked into the dealership and made enough noise to ensure that the other two could hear us in the building. I knew nothing could ever make Bobby feel uncomfortable, but in some twisted way I wanted Elaine to feel uncomfortable with Bobby. It was then that I heard Bobby say "Shhhh!" and Katie screamed and let out a little giggle. Within seconds, a disheveled Bobby appeared looking as though he had thrown his clothes on. It was exactly what I wanted Elaine to see. I could see the outline of Katie's body in Bobby's darkened office struggling to get her clothes on and I silently hoped that Elaine was noticing that as well. To drive the point home, I left Elaine standing there where she could see Bobby's office and walked away to speak with Bobby about the fax that had indeed come in that afternoon.

As we walked into my office, we both heard Katie call out "Bobby, where are you?" She then added, "I need your help. My hair is stuck in my zipper."

Neither woman noticed that we were already watching and as we got closer I witnessed a side of Elaine I would have never imagined possible. She was attempting to help Katie free her hair from the zipper and after only a second or two, Elaine was able to get the zipper down. As she did, she pulled quite a few of Katie's bleached blonde hairs from the back of her head. It was quite obvious to me that Elaine had done it on purpose and while I was no fan of Katie, I was still a little shocked at my girlfriend's behavior. As nonchalant as I had ever seen her, Elaine quickly feigned an apology "Oh! I am so sorry! Did that hurt?"

Bobby and I looked at each other and both struggled not to laugh out loud. We walked over toward Bobby's office where the girls were standing and we both left the office with our 'dates'. I was again left with that same uneasy feeling that Elaine had some very real feelings for Bobby. Seeing the dynamic of the two women together definitely had an impact. Of course, I never would ask Elaine about what I had seen because I was afraid of what her answer might be.

Chapter Nine

The following morning, Bobby and I left for Philadelphia. We had made plans to drive to there to pick up a very important car that Bobby had made a very impressive deal for. Bobby had been owed a favor for several years by the owner of a car auction business there. The auctioneer and Bobby had talked a week earlier and Bobby was able to finally call in his favor. Bobby had struck a deal to buy a 1973 Dodge Challenger in mint condition. The car looked almost identical to the car Bobby had owned while we were in high school. I knew from the beginning that this car would never be sold at the dealership. Bobby took more money from his rainy day fund and arranged the purchase. It was never my intention to make money on the deal. I wanted to have fun on a road trip with Bobby. It was a six and a half hour drive and with weekday traffic it took us just short of seven hours. Bobby was extremely excited and I thought to myself, "Why shouldn't he be?"

He had won the tournament the day before, he was on his way to again having the car that was his first love, AND he had no less than a hundred women in his club. He definitely had every right to be happy. Who wouldn't be? As for me, I was happy to be spending time with my best friend again. We drove. We talked. We laughed. We snacked on food we normally didn't eat. Bobby loved road trips with me. Since he had married Dana, his diet had been limited due to her food allergies. Things like nuts were not even allowed in their house. Not only that, but he couldn't eat nuts at work and go home and kiss her. I always teased Bobby about 'the kiss of death' and the fact that Dana could not tolerate any 'nuts' in her mouth. We laughed wildly about all of it while we were together. With Dana, he was very careful at her request and was happy to abide by her rules. At least until he hit the open road and was away from home for a few days. Then, all bets were off. Cashews. Macadamias. Pistachios. No nut was safe. It was so easy to predict. Get Bobby away from home and he would eat anything that had a nut in it. It was so ridiculous it was silly.

By the time we got to the auctioneer's dealership it had closed for the day. That really didn't matter to us as we had planned to spend the night at a hotel before driving home anyway.

The drive had been tiresome for both of us but we still had enough energy to find an appetite for a nice steak dinner courtesy of The Lottery Club girls. "My treat. Out of my rainy day fund, the sky is the limit!" Bobby joked as we were seated by the restaurant host. Our waitress appeared moments later asking for our drink order, and her looks didn't go unnoticed by either of us. She was very young and extremely sexy. Bobby wasted no time pouring on the charm.

Over dinner, we reminisced and we laughed. Elizabeth came up during conversation because the last time we had seen her had been in the nearby town of Scranton. We talked about the tennis tournament Bobby had won the day before and Bobby thanked me for letting him win. We both laughed very hard about that and knew it was for the best that we let all of that go.

Obviously, we talked about The Lottery Club. We were having fun and laughing until suddenly I saw a light go off in Bobby's head and he looked at me and said "Shit. I left my lottery ticket at home and I still need to send a picture of it to some of The Lottery Club members."

"So now what?" I asked him

"Relax. I got it covered." Bobby smiled his usual smile and I knew he meant it.

Bobby then excused himself from our table explaining that he had to make a phone call. I found this unusual and was curious as to who he would be calling that he wasn't willing to talk with in front of me. Normally, Bobby never felt a real need for privacy with his calls and I started imagining that it must be Elaine that he was calling. After about seven or eight minutes had passed, Bobby returned to our table and we picked up our conversation without skipping a beat. We finished our dinner and dessert as I continued drinking one beer after the other knowing I didn't have to drive anywhere that night. Bobby drank cup after cup of coffee. Eventually, it was necessary to excuse myself from the table to find a bathroom. When I returned, Bobby stood up with the announcement that the coffee was running right through him. With that he was gone, leaving his phone on the table directly across from me. I am embarrassed to say so, but perhaps it was my obsession with Elaine that drove me to consider invading Bobby's privacy. I knew that all I had to do was ask and I was a hundred percent sure Bobby would tell me the truth. However, something about actually doing that made me feel vulnerable and I knew Bobby well enough to know I would run the risk of him telling me I was 'pussy whipped' for needing to know if he had talked with Elaine. I looked down at his phone for a split second and then looked around the restaurant. Our waitress was busy at another table and the few people left in the restaurant at that hour were all seemingly engrossed in their own conversations. I reached quickly across the table for Bobby's phone. Fortunately, Bobby and I had the same kind of phone, so it was easy for me to look natural as I searched for what I needed to know. I swiped through a couple screens and I found the information I was looking for, sort of. There had been a couple of texts that I did not bother to read, but Bobby had not made any calls since we had gotten to the restaurant. What had he been doing?

I carefully put the phone back on the table where Bobby had left it. I was unwilling to explore further for fear of being caught looking at Bobby's phone.

Bobby returned to the table and behind him the waitress arrived with our check. Bobby had continued to flirt with her throughout the evening and he didn't seem ready to stop. He paid the bill with cash and leaned toward the waitress and handed her something that I assumed was the tip.

On our way back to the hotel, Bobby laughed and said "I wonder if she'll actually show up." I wasn't sure I knew what he was talking about and when I asked, he laughed and said "Never mind."

I realized what was going on the moment Bobby went to the front desk at the hotel and explained that he had lost his key card to his room. Bobby had obviously given his key to the waitress as he had handed her the tip. In the elevator I noticed Bobby looking at his new key and smirking. I assured Bobby that she would show up, no question. "She will be a member of the lottery club before morning." I added as we walked out of the elevator onto our floor.

Bobby laughed and said "50-50 chance."

I knew it was more like a 99.9% chance. We each headed toward the doors to our adjacent rooms and I laughed and told Bobby "Don't be up all night. We have a long drive back."

Bobby reminded me that I was the one that was having difficulty enunciating my words and maintaining a vertical posture. He, on the other hand, hadn't had one drop of alcohol. He assured me, as usual, that he had it covered. We agreed to leave at eight the next morning and we said goodnight.

As it turned out, the waitress did come up to his room that night. The next morning, right on schedule at five minutes to eight I was knocking on Bobby's door. He opened the door and let me inside. Bobby was ready to go but I could hear that the shower was running. Bobby leaned into the bathroom and said "Goodbye Sara" to the girl in the shower and reminded her to be sure to send the pictures of her lottery tickets twice a week. We walked out the door towards the elevator and I couldn't help laughing at my friend.

As the doors closed behind us I said, "I told you she would come."

Bobby, in his twisted way, smiled and said "Oh, believe me, she did. More than once."

I shook my head and changed the subject to the business at hand. "Are you ready to go pick up your baby?" I asked, referring of course to the car.

At the same time, Bobby was looking at his phone and had completely tuned me out. It seemed to take him a second or two to process whatever it was he was looking at on the phone but it was obvious that something was very wrong. Bobby looked as white as a ghost as he gasped and fumbled with the phone to call a number. As he did, he held up his hand for me to be quiet. He had switched his phone back to the text as he waited for someone to answer. I could now see the text on his phone. I could see his hands shaking as he read it over again. "I found your lottery ticket. You hit the jackpot! Call me!!!" Bobby was calling his wife.

It took what seemed like forever for her to answer her phone. To say that Bobby was agitated by the time she did so would be a massive understatement.

He tried to sound calm but it was clear that he was upset. "Where did you find the ticket and what in the world even possessed you to check the numbers?" he demanded.

In the small confines of the elevator I heard her answer. She told him that she had started doing laundry that morning and she found the ticket in one of his pockets. "I thought it was unusual, knowing that you *never* play the lottery. I was surprised to find the ticket so I decided to check the numbers. When I did, every number matched!" She was now shouting and, unlike Bobby, she sounded happy about it.

105

Bobby was becoming more and more upset as the reality of the situation began to settle in. He talked to Dana and tried in vain to get her attention. When he was finally able to get her to focus and listen to him, he said "Listen to me. This is very important. DO NOT tell anyone about this until I get home. It will probably be another seven hours until I can be there. This is very important. You can tell absolutely NO ONE."

There was dead silence on both ends of the phone for about ten seconds. I nearly jumped out of my skin when I finally heard Bobby bark at her "Do you understand me? Are you there?"

The one word response shook Bobby, it was in that one moment of hesitation he knew everything he was afraid to know.

"Why?" she asked.

"You need to trust me on this. If anyone at all finds out about this before I have the chance to take care of a few things this will turn out very badly for us."

The silence on the other end again spoke volumes and Bobby was ready to crawl out of his skin.

He screamed at her, "Do you understand what I am saying?"

I heard her begin to cry and then came the apology. "I am sorry. I wanted to tell someone. I told Stacey."

I had never seen Bobby react this way in any situation. I didn't know what to do. I suddenly wished that I was somewhere else. Anywhere else would have been perfect. Bobby slammed his hand so hard against the mirrored finish of the stainless steel that the entire elevator shook. Bobby looked as if someone had stabbed him through the heart and he gasped, "God damn it, this is going to get really bad."

Dana's sister was a television reporter with the local network and Bobby had always said, "If you want to keep a secret, don't tell Stacey." Bobby and I were a good six and a half hours away from home and by now the story was all over the news. The ticket Bobby's wife was now holding was one of only two tickets that would split the $450 million jackpot. The details were well known. There was, of course, the ticket Bobby's wife now had. That ticket had been purchased in Buffalo. The other ticket was not nearly as newsworthy and there seemed to be no interest at all in the ticket that had been purchased just hours before the drawing in another state.

Bobby still had his wife on the phone and was working hard at convincing her how important it was to him that she not talk with anyone else or take any phone calls from anyone until he could get home. He pleaded with her to get in her car and drive to her mother's house in Rochester with the ticket. He promised that he would be there as soon as he possibly could.

She repeated her apology and agreed to drive to Rochester. Bobby ended the call. Bobby looked to me like a man whose world was collapsing in around him.

I didn't know what to say. From my mouth came the same question I had asked before the call, "Are you ready to go pick up your baby?" It was the most absurd question to ask. I already knew the answer.

"Fuck that car. We have to go NOW."

What I really wanted to say to Bobby was, "I thought you had this covered." Fortunately, I caught myself before the words left my mouth. Maybe I felt like he had been asking for this. I knew he was playing with fire and now Bobby was getting burned. I almost didn't feel bad, but he was my friend and it wasn't the time to jab him for making questionable decisions.

In as much of a hurry as Bobby was to get home, we made one stop before we started toward Rochester. For reasons I didn't understand, Bobby needed to stop at a post office. We found one that was only a couple blocks from the hotel. He ran inside while I waited in the car for about two minutes before he jumped back in and we drove to the freeway.

Bobby insisted on driving the entire drive to Rochester. He drove so recklessly and so fast that I honestly felt in fear for my life. Bobby was driving like a stunt car driver. He was weaving in and out of traffic, cutting people off, and passing cars and trucks on the shoulder of the road.

By now, Bobby's wife had left their house for the drive to her mother's house. On her way, she drove past the dealership where there were two news vans sitting and waiting for the dealership to open under the assumption that they would find Bobby there. Things were quickly getting out of hand.

Chapter Ten

We made the trip in about four and a half hours; a solid forty five minutes less than it should have taken us. Even then, we were too late. It had been less than six hours since his wife had discovered the ticket. By now, even her mother's house was surrounded by reporters and camera crews. Bobby's lottery win was a secret to no one.

Several members of the lottery club already knew about the win and had started coming forward. The madness that had begun that morning and the insanity of Bobby's new reality that would soon follow was completely surreal. What was happening was so totally unimaginable that I gave up trying to guess what might happen next.

We parked the car outside Dana's mother's house and Bobby began fighting his way through the sea of people that had gathered in attempt to reach the front door. Bobby was shouting at everyone around him as he pushed people out of his way, "Why don't you mind your own business and go report some real news!"

He finally made it through the crowd and managed to get inside the house. Seconds after Bobby had closed the door behind him, reporters had surrounded the car I was sitting in while waiting for Bobby. They screamed questions at me as though I would answer.

Over the next few hours, the story gained a life of its own. Wherever there were people talking, they were talking about Bobby. And everyone was anxious for every little detail they could learn about The Lottery Club.

For the first time in my life, I no longer wished for what Bobby had. As I sat alone inside the parked car outside his in-laws' house in the fancy upscale suburb of Rochester, I could only imagine the drama that was being played out inside the house. Dana's parents had always been judgmental when it came to Bobby, extending all the way back to his days of abusing drugs and alcohol. That, combined with the newest rumors of extramarital affairs, I was quite sure that things were probably not going Bobby's way. I would later learn that during the time he was inside, Bobby had been told by Dana that he absolutely needed to be out of the house they shared by 9am the next morning. According to Bobby, it had gone something like, "Get your things out of my house and don't you ever come back. I mean it, Bobby. I want you gone. Forever." Dana informed Bobby that she would 'appreciate' it if he was not around to cause her any more problems than he already had. What followed her seemingly legitimate request was a series of heated discussions and arguments between the two of them. At one point, Dana's father interjected with the demand that either Bobby leave immediately and on his own free will or that an officer or two that had arrived outside to control the growing crowd would be invited in to remove Bobby from the property. Bobby demanded the lottery ticket from Dana and insisted that there was no way he was leaving without the winning ticket. Dana refused and Bobby began losing his temper.

"None of this would have happened if you would have just minded your own business and let me handle things!" Bobby shouted at her in complete frustration.

With this, Dana's father immediately summoned the police into his home and requested that Bobby be removed from the property. As he was being forcibly removed, Bobby again screamed at Dana, "You ruined everything! I had a plan and you were a part of it!"

When Bobby was outside the door he turned back toward Dana who was now standing in the doorway. Bobby gathered his composure and for a split second attempted a last ditch effort to use his charm on the woman he had promised himself to forever. "Please, Baby, just give me the lottery ticket and I will take care of everything."

Dana, on the other hand, was as angry as ever and looked at the man she had promised to love forever and said, "Over my dead body."

The calmness was gone from Bobby's face and the anger welled up again. As he stood in front of the house with a sea of reporters at his back, in a voice as loud and clear as any before, Bobby proclaimed "Good. If that's the way it's going to be, so be it."

The door slammed as Bobby turned toward the car and with the police officers on either side of him he began walking through the crowd as they screamed questions at him.

At the time, few could have predicted the storm that would follow those few words said in anger and recorded by one news crew that afternoon. That one news outlet was immediately reporting the incident as a threat to Dana's life. This was clearly not the case and nothing could have been further from the truth. In reality, the meaning of Bobby's words was quite simply, "I guess we'll have to do this the hard way." It was perhaps just a poor choice of wording that Bobby used to let her know that he had every intention of using the law to get his ticket from her. Understandably, Bobby was full of rage and was obviously not thinking clearly. With his legal background it is almost too easy to say that Bobby knew better than to say something like that. Either way, the exchange would come back to bite Bobby in the ass.

When Bobby got back into the car and settled himself into the seat, he looked over at me with his usual smirk and announced, "Well that went better than I expected." We both laughed and decided to drive back to Buffalo to face the full fury that had commenced that day with the exposure of The Lottery Club.

We drove to the dealership and as we slowed the car to pull in, we noticed the two news vans laying in wait for Bobby. It was about a quarter after three in the afternoon and we both needed to get inside. He immediately removed his foot from the break and hit the gas. It was an instantaneous decision by Bobby to not pull into the dealership in front of all the cameras. It was an effort to avoid drawing the nearly unavoidable attention of the reporters. I agreed with his decision and we went to one of the side streets where we could get inside through the service department undetected. I think Bobby wanted to go inside to see if there were any messages and to find out exactly how far things had gotten out of control at the dealership.

The receptionist walked toward us as we quickly approached Bobby's office. She smiled and said "There are obviously a bunch of messages for you, but the two most important ones are that Katie stopped in to log in a few cars and your cleaning lady, Maggie, came by to tell you personally that 'You are an ass hole and I quit.'"

Bobby smiled at her and said "No argument here. Thank you."

Bobby hurried into his office and tapped on his computer keyboard. "Oh shit! I really am an ass hole. I left The Lottery Club program open. I am glad we came by just for that reason. I can't believe it's been open all this time."

He closed the program and looked at me saying, "It is at least as bad as I expected if not worse."

By then, the reporters had started looking in the windows and we decided it was time to make a hasty retreat.

We walked back out through the same door we had used to get inside and got into the car without anyone taking notice. We drove from the dealership and agreed to wait until closing time at 6pm and return sometime after that to go inside and take care of a few business matters that each of us had pending.

Bobby's cell phone was ringing again. It hadn't stopped ringing since the story broke. This time, like dozens of times before, Bobby held up his phone where I could see the name of the caller and each time it was another member of the club. "Becky TLC" had called no less than three times. "Jen TLC" refused to leave a message and every time she tried to call and he wouldn't answer she would immediately try again. It was so completely out of control. As time passed, more and more girls were finding out and it seemed that the phone was constantly ringing, receiving a text or recording a voicemail. Some of the girls seemed to think that maybe an email would work and even that alert was beginning to make me crazy. Every one of them wanted to know what was going on and more than one seemed to be strangely happy about being part of the mess that had been created. I wondered to myself why he didn't just put the phone on silent or turn it off completely, but Bobby also seemed to be enjoying the chaos that he had created for himself. I think that I would have been horrified had I been in Bobby's shoes, but Bobby wasn't missing a beat. He seemed to be in an incredibly good mood for someone that had just been tossed from his happy home. He was definitely acting more like someone that had just won the lottery and didn't have a care left in the world.

We managed to keep a low profile and it was just after 6pm when we again approached the dealership. It appeared as though the news crews had given up, at least for the day, and had packed up their cameras and left. Bobby parked the car and we both went inside to our respective offices. We both had business to take care of and there was no doubt in my mind that Bobby needed to get to his rainy day fund that he had kept stashed away in his office.

I went into my office to deal with whatever it was that I had missed in the two days I had been out. Surprisingly, there were only two voicemails and a handful of emails I needed to respond to. I got through it all quickly as I glanced back and forth at the plain white envelope lying on my desk. It had caught my eye the moment I had walked into my office and switched on the light. It was clear to me by the handwriting the hand that had so beautifully written "Denny" across the front of the envelope. It was from Elaine. I was afraid to open it. It was unusual to get something like this from Elaine. I fought to believe it was some little romantic gesture she had made while Bobby and I had been away. Maybe it was some playful invitation from her. Perhaps it was just a beautiful letter saying things she couldn't say to me in person. Or perhaps it was an awful letter explaining things she couldn't say to me in person. My heart sank and a knot formed in my stomach as the feeling rushed over me that the latter was true.

I got up from my desk and walked with the unopened envelope into Bobby's office. I knew I would need the support of my friend if the letter really contained what it was that I was afraid it held.

The scope of the effect The Lottery Club was having on Bobby's life was obvious as I looked at the glass walls of Bobby's office. The receptionist had made a habit of writing Bobby's messages on the back of post-it notes and then sticking them to the glass. It was out of courtesy for him that it was done this way so she never had to interrupt him during a phone call or when he was with people in his office. Today, the glass was so covered with notes that it was almost impossible to see inside the office. In contrast, there had been one post-it note on my window. One little yellow note alerting me to the fact that Elaine had come in and left the letter for me at 3:15 that afternoon.

When I stepped into his office I could see that every one held virtually the same message. They were all from women in the Lottery Club. "Call Susan," followed by a phone number. "Call Jackie" followed by the message, "Urgent." Again and again and again. Message after message. Everyone seemed impatient and determined to talk with Bobby. There had also been a message stuck to his computer screen saying, "I logged in a couple of used cars. Call me when you get a chance Cassanova. Love, Katie."

I noticed that the lottery ticket he had taped to his computer the very day of the club's conception was gone. In that moment I assumed that Katie must have taken it as some kind of a weird momento.

He looked up to acknowledge me standing in the doorway and motioned to all the notes on the glass. "Crazy, isn't it?"

I shook my head and agreed. I held up the envelope to show Bobby and I half-heartedly joked with him as I opened the envelope saying, "What do you think this is all about?"

Bobby replied, "There's only one way to find out. What does it say?"

I pulled the paper from the envelope and unfolded it with shaky hands as my head reeled with the possibilities of what I might read. The first time through it was like I hadn't even read it. My mind focused on the page and all the important words hit me like a freight train. I read it again slowly as Bobby waited. To me, this was the worst news imaginable. This one single paper held the end of all my hopes and dreams of a life shared with Elaine. The short letter explained that she could no longer see me anymore and did not want to hurt my feelings by continuing to string me along. She said that she recognized the fact that the feelings I had for her were much stronger than the feelings she had for me and that she saw no real future for the two of us. I felt hurt, but I somehow had known from the beginning that this was true. I had only wished to prolong it as long as I possibly could. My heart was breaking and as I reached the end of the letter, the last line said "Tell Bobby that maybe I will see him around sometime." It was signed "Love, Elaine." Elaine had indeed used the letter to tell me things that she couldn't tell me in person.

I folded the letter and put it back in the envelope. I wasn't sure what to do with it. Part of me wanted to toss it in the little waste paper basket next to Bobby's desk. I wasn't ready to let go. I folded the envelope and carefully put it in my pocket.

"Well that was crappy timing." I said to Bobby. I didn't believe it had anything to do with The Lottery Club, but "Hell," I thought, "When it rains it pours."

Although it didn't show, I knew that Bobby's troubles were far worse than mine. Since he was at a point where he had nothing to do and nowhere to go, I extended an invitation to go out to eat or perhaps to go over to the tennis club. I thought it might do us both some good to take out a little aggression on some tennis balls. Not surprisingly, Bobby declined my offer saying that he wanted to be alone for a while to figure out his next move. I expressed my concern and asked him what he planned to do.

"Go have fun. Don't worry. I got it covered."

By then it was already 6:30 and I desperately needed to put my mind on something else. I really wanted Bobby to come with me, but there is zero chance of changing Bobby's mind once he has decided on something. I left the dealership and left Bobby alone with his thoughts. I also knew from our earlier conversation that he had been given until 9am to get whatever he needed from the house at which time he was expected by Dana to be out of her life 'forever'.

It wasn't until later that I found out what Bobby had done in the time after I left the dealership that evening until the time he checked into a hotel room a few minutes after midnight.

Bobby told me that he had left soon after I did and drove over to his house to retrieve a couple changes of clothes and his favorite tennis racquet. It took a matter of minutes at which point he had tossed his house keys onto the kitchen counter and walked out of the house.

After leaving the house, Bobby had then made the decision to find Elaine that night. I want to believe that Bobby would not have gone to see her if I hadn't gotten the letter that day. I was having a difficult time convincing myself that there was nothing either romantic or sexual between Elaine and Bobby. Bobby had been my friend forever, but now I was especially jealous of the friendship that I was certain still remained between Bobby and Elaine. Neither of them had ever given me a reason to believe that there was anything between them and I sure as hell wanted to believe that was the case. Now that the letter existed, I had some very persistent doubts about whatever relationship Elaine and I had shared. Regardless of what decisions she had made, I still loved her. I felt jealous of the fact that Bobby even felt as though he could show up at her house to see her. I wanted to see her.

My mind kept wandering back to the fact that neither of us had heard anything from Elaine. There had been no texts. There had been no calls. It was beginning to feel, at least to me, as if she had suddenly disappeared from the face of the earth. I was having a tough time wrapping my mind around it. For some reason, my best friend, whose disposition seemed extraordinarily good in spite of his issues with Dana, drove to see the woman that had been my girlfriend up until a few hours earlier. Bobby kept saying, "If it wasn't meant to be, it wasn't meant to be." I had immediately begun work on convincing myself of that. Perhaps he was right, perhaps it wasn't meant to be. His logic wasn't working for me and I fought hard against the wisdom that may have freed me from the hurt Elaine was causing.

Whatever his reasons were for going, Bobby made the forty minute drive to the Buffalo suburb of Clarence where Elaine lived to see her that night. When he got to the house, it was totally dark and Elaine's car was not in the driveway. He later explained that he had arrived and waited until almost 11:30 for Elaine to come back to her house. She never did. I guess that wasn't meant to be either, because Bobby drove the back roads all the way back and spent the night at a hotel near the dealership.

The next day was a beautiful sunny day that somehow seemed clouded by the constant news reports about Bobby and The Lottery Club. Not surprisingly, a few more women had stepped forward for their fifteen minutes of fame. A few discussed their individual arrangements with Bobby. Some of them talked about their 'personal' relationships with Bobby as well. Each woman had a slightly different story from the others but every one of them had one thing in common, The Lottery Club.

I had arrived for work early that morning for a meeting I had asked to have with my father. I wanted to talk with him about an idea I had for recovering some normalcy to our car lot. Dad and I both agreed that although a little publicity would be good for sales, this situation had the potential for getting out of hand very quickly. We feared that the constant presence of reporters might disrupt our business. Living in the same town my whole life and working at my family's generations old dealership had its benefits. I made the decision to call in a favor to a friend at the county sheriff's department. We were able to make arrangements to keep news crews and reporters off the dealership property. The fact that Bobby planned to continue to show up at work was bound to be a liability with the news frenzy that was now surrounding him. We were only a day in and it was easy to imagine that it wasn't going to die down anytime soon. My dad was so impressed with the way I got out ahead of the disaster that was about to strike that I don't believe he will ever stop talking about my foresight with regard to the situation.

I had been in my office for nearly an hour that morning when Bobby showed up. He was looking remarkably good considering he was now, for all intents and purposes, living in a hotel room that was a world apart from the lavish home he had shared with Dana. Bobby looked great. He walked into the building smiling and whistling and appearing the happiest that I had seen him in many years. My first thought was that maybe the exposure of The Lottery Club had lifted a weight from his shoulders. It was clear to me that he was acting as confident as ever. I had every confidence that Bobby would be able to turn things around as he always had. Legal degree or no legal degree, with Bobby's legal prowess it seemed to be a foregone conclusion that he would somehow manage to get his hands on at least part of his lottery jackpot.

I got up from my desk and walked out to greet him. I gave him the old knuckle bump and walked with him to his office. It felt like normal again. I was joking with him and he was teasing me. He opened the door to his office and started straightening things on his desk. He reached down and picked up the poster of Dana from the floor and was putting it back on the wall. I asked him what had happened and Bobby laughed and said, "Katie made me take it down the night we were here after the tennis tournament. I guess it made her uncomfortable to have Dana watch while I was banging her." Just then, two officers walked into the office. I started to ask them about the press as I assumed it must have something to do with that but they dismissed me and demanded Bobby's attention. The taller of the two men addressed Bobby first.

"Are you Robert Ferrari?"

Bobby responded in the affirmative and the officer asked Bobby to please come with them outside. Bobby jokingly asked them "Do I have a choice?" thinking it must have something to do with The Lottery Club.

"As a matter of fact, you do not." The officer responded.

Bobby asked the two officers if they could at least tell him what this was all about, but the officers would only say that they had been instructed to bring him back to the Ferrari residence.

The whole situation seemed wrong and suddenly the lighthearted banter Bobby and I had shared that morning was over. I made the decision to follow the officers as they took Bobby to the house. I admit it had more to do with personal curiosity than anything else at that point. I thought that maybe Dana had accused him of doing something stupid with regard to the house.

As we drove toward the house, I could see that was not the case at all. My first impression of the situation was that it felt so surreal. It looked like something from a movie. There were several police cars, both marked and unmarked, in the driveway. In addition to the police, there was one ambulance parked close to the house. There were neighbors and news reporters standing in the street and it appeared as though the entire property had been taped off with the yellow tape. "Crime Scene Do Not Enter".

I pulled up right behind the patrol car. We all got out of the cars and I asked if it was okay for me to stay with Bobby. They informed me that it may not be a great idea but left the decision to Bobby. Bobby instructed them that he wanted me with him.

We walked up the driveway and were greeted by two detectives, one male and one female. The male detective was Mike Dayton. Bobby and I had gone to school with him and had most recently seen him at the tennis tournament only days earlier. The other detective was an extremely attractive 35-ish woman that had dated Bobby before he had married Dana. Mike looked serious and at that moment somewhat formally confirmed that Bobby was indeed Robert Ferrari 'for the record'. My heart sank as I knew this was not about Bobby having taken something that Dana didn't want him to have. It was apparent that Bobby was in some real trouble this time.

Bobby looked angry as he said to Mike "Stop fucking around, Mike, you know who I am! What is going on?!"

"Dana is dead, Bobby" Mike said very matter-of-factly. The full meaning hadn't settled on either of us as Bobby noticed Dana's parents being escorted from the house after having been asked to identify the body. Bobby had no time to react to anything that was happening before Dana's mother's eyes fixed on Bobby in the driveway. In that moment, she lost all control and stormed over to where Bobby was still standing in disbelief. The female detective, Kelly, did all she could to restrain the older woman but she continued to scream hysterically at Bobby in a piercing voice that sent chills down my spine.

"You bastard! My baby is dead! You said you would kill her and now my baby is dead!"

The officers carried her from the scene but as they did she continued to cry and scream obscenities at Bobby.

The news cameras were all rolling and every reporter there, whether from print or tv, was eating up every horrible detail of the day.

Bobby hadn't moved. The sparkle was gone from his eyes and in its place was a look of terror. He stood staring toward the door where his in-laws had just walked out moments before. It was clear that the shock and disbelief had taken hold of him as he kept repeating, "What happened? What are you all talking about? There is no way Dana is dead. No. This is not possible."

After a few minutes, the situation seemed to sink in a little with Bobby and I saw the tears in his eyes as he demanded to see Dana.

The officers requested that I wait outside and I was happy to oblige as they walked with Bobby into the house. There were teams of investigators inside taking pictures and collecting evidence. There was so much forensic evidence being collected that Bobby was forbidden from actually going into the kitchen where Dana's body lay on the cold porcelain tile floor.

"I want you to know that this is being treated as a murder." Mike said to Bobby who continued to look nothing short of confused about what was going on around him.

"What are you talking about? Murder?" Bobby demanded as he pushed his way toward the kitchen doorway.

The detective grabbed Bobby by the arm and told him that the details were in no way clear at the time, but it appeared as though Dana's death had been caused by a severe allergic reaction.

"Mike, what are you talking about? Just because she died from an allergic reaction to something doesn't mean it was murder. You know as well as I do that Dana is highly allergic to nuts and even the slightest contact with any type of nuts could have killed her."

Mike said, "Bobby, I understand that but her Epi-Pen had been super glued closed. She apparently died trying to open it and give herself an injection, as gruesome as that may be."

The officers brought Bobby back outside where they began questioning him. It was obvious to me that Bobby was in no condition to be answering the questions they were asking. I immediately joined the group and as they asked about his whereabouts I quickly provided an alibi for the day before by stating that I had been with Bobby all day up until I left the dealership at 6:30pm. This was not enough to satisfy the police and they asked Bobby where he had been between the hours of 6:30 pm until 10 am that day. Bobby's response was a half hearted reply "I checked into a hotel and spent the night there alone."

I was concerned that this was all too much for my friend to be dealing with, but the officers explained that they would need more details from him. Mike explained that due to the circumstances and the fact that Bobby was unable to provide an alibi for the night before that he was going to have to place Bobby under arrest for the murder of Dana Ferrari.

The officer read him his rights and asked Bobby if he understood his rights. Bobby nodded and quietly said "yes" as they cuffed him. Bobby was in such shock that the men had to practically carry him to the car as he was unable to walk. He looked unlike any incarnation of Bobby that I had ever known. My mind wasn't able to process what I was seeing. I can't begin to imagine what was going on inside Bobby's head. I kept thinking to myself that Bobby had netted $105 million in the lottery just 24 hours before and tonight his wife was dead and he had been charged with her murder. How could anybody possibly wrap their head around that?

Whoever thought that winning the lottery could turn out so bad.

Chapter Eleven

Within a few hours, the video of Dana's mother at the scene was all over the news adding visual and audio effects to the story of Dana's death. They were reporting that she had been murdered and that Bobby had been charged. In typical fashion, the reporters, in order to sensationalize the news had given a name to the story. They had picked up on the name "The Lottery Club" and Bobby was now "The Lottery Club Killer".

The media was truly eating this up. They had edited together a loop of the footage beginning with Dana saying "over my dead body", with Bobby's response "If that's the way it's going to be, so be it", followed by the footage of Dana's mother screaming and accusing Bobby of killing her daughter.

The questioning went on for Bobby down at the station. It wasn't looking good for him. The interrogator was drilling him about the hotel and accusing him of lying to police. Since they now had proof that Bobby had checked into the hotel at precisely 12:22 am the morning of the murder, they called his statement at the scene a lie. In reality, Bobby had stated only that he had checked into the hotel and spent the night alone. He had never actually provided them with a timeline. I found it quite upsetting that his simple answer to a question asked just minutes after learning that his wife had been killed was now being held against him in this way. Bobby had answered their question truthfully but not in detail and it was obvious to all that had been there that Bobby had been in shock at the time. In any event, before the day was through, Bobby had been arraigned and the presiding judge had set bail at $200,000.

In the back of mind I wondered if Bobby was capable of doing such a thing. I recalled a time long ago when Bobby's dad had been accused of attempted murder. I remember thinking that there was no possible way his dad could have done something like that. As it turned out, I was wrong. I entertained the thought in my head that I might be wrong about Bobby as well.

It was around 9pm when my phone rang and snapped me out of my thoughts and back into reality. It was Bobby's voice on the phone. He was using his one phone call and he was calling me. It was a stupid question but I asked him if he was okay.

"Not really," he said, "I need you to go to my rainy day fund and get $200,000 for bail money. When you have it, please come and get me."

I told Bobby I would do that if he promised to answer one question truthfully for me. He agreed. I asked if he had killed Dana or if he had anything to do with it. I immediately felt embarrassed and heartbroken that I had asked my friend such a thing. At the same time, I was afraid to know the answer if the answer was 'yes'. I wasn't sure at the time what my reaction would be. It almost seemed like a threat and that I was insinuating that I wouldn't help him if I didn't hear an answer I liked. Then again, I wondered if I would really believe him if the answer was 'no'. I did a lot of thinking in that one moment as I waited for his answer. I suddenly wished I had not even asked the question.

When Bobby responded with, "How could you even think that I had anything at all to do with it?" I felt like the worst friend anyone has ever had. He continued by saying, "You have known me my whole life." I felt that I had betrayed my best friend at the time when he needed me the most.

I told him that I was sorry and that he did not need to answer.

Bobby thanked me and then proceeded to answer my question. He said that he wanted there to be no doubt in my mind, ever. He told me unequivocally "No."

That was all I needed to hear. I would never doubt Bobby again. He started to ask again about the money and I cut him short.

"I got it covered."

I heard Bobby laugh quietly to himself and I think it comforted him to hear me using his words.

"I will be there as early as I can tomorrow. Try to rest." I said as we prepared to end the conversation.

I put my phone down and swore under my breath. What had possessed me to ask Bobby that question? I was Bobby's best friend. I was the one he had called and I was sounding as if I had doubts about him. Anyway, Bobby was too smart to say something that would incriminate him on a police station phone. The fact was, I believed him when he said he had nothing to do with Dana's murder. I was disappointed in myself for asking the question.

The next morning I went to my dad and had a check for $200,000 within the hour. By the time all the paperwork was done, Bobby had spent a little more than a day in the county jail.

Within that short period of time more than ninety women had come forward to make their claim on the winning lottery ticket. Every hour on every channel there were the faces of countless women with their stories about Bobby. Some of the women were bold enough to talk about their personal and sexual relationships with Bobby. It seemed as if each wanted to out-do the other with the stories of Bobby's sexual exploits. They were more than eager to share details with the reporters and all of them appeared to genuinely enjoy their time in the spotlight. As Bobby's friend, I found this disturbing and rather tasteless. Surprisingly as it may seem, they all had good things to say about Bobby but more importantly they all certainly wanted a cut of the money.

Several of the women were already forming an organization, another club of sorts, and they were planning to sue Bobby. Many of the women had come to the conclusion that they wanted to get out ahead of everything and everyone else and make a grab for whatever they could get. They determined that by banding together and pooling their resources it would be easier.

When I picked Bobby up at the jail, he was holding stacks of legal papers. Most were individual notices that that nearly every member of The Lottery Club had filed a lawsuit against Bobby, both individually and as a group. Bobby was overly emotional and was nearly choked to tears as he told me that his in-laws had also filed a wrongful death lawsuit against him in Dana's death. He did not mince his words as he explained that he was upset with the fact that Dana had only been dead a couple days and they were already filing lawsuits. They had wasted no time grieving and had instead decided to go after as much money as they could get.

I asked Bobby what he planned to do about all the civil lawsuits that were already in the process of being filed against him as well as the more pressing legal matter of having been charged with the actual murder.

"I have absolutely no intention of contesting the civil lawsuits. I will file 'no contest' and the courts can do what they want with the money. Speaking of money, obviously you had no problem getting the money from my rainy day fund to cover bail?"

When I told Bobby that I had asked my Dad for the money and he had instantly written the check for $200,000 it looked as though Bobby was going to cry. Clearly, Bobby was overwhelmed as though a vote of confidence had been given to him by my father.

Bobby then asked if we could stop at the dealership. He wanted to see if there was anything left in his office, specifically the money. The night of the arrest, a search warrant had been issued and the police had gone through Bobby's office. We arrived and he ran to the file cabinet where he had tucked the money under the bottom drawer. He pulled the drawer out and there was the money. He had already put the $10,000 back that he had taken for his car in Pennsylvania. He took that envelope and another $5,000 and handed the balance to me.

"Here," he said, "This is the $200,000 to give to your dad to pay back the bail money he gave me."

I took the money from him knowing that the least I could do was to keep Bobby's money in a safe place for him.

Bobby and I drove back to my house. Shortly after we had settled in, Bobby finally broke down and confided in me that he didn't care what happened to him anymore. He cried as he told me that nothing mattered to him and that as far as he was concerned, they could find him guilty, lock him up and throw away the key.

I was shocked to hear him saying things like that. I wanted Bobby to fight. We both knew that he didn't do it. I wanted him, for his own sake, to let the world know he was not a murderer.

I asked him to please give it some thought. I then insisted that he eat some real food and told him that no way was I going to take 'no' for an answer. We went to our favorite local steakhouse where I knew the owner. We were hoping to avoid any and all attention and I knew it would be a quiet place. The owner brought us in through the back door and seated us at one of the tables in back. There were one or two tables that noticed us and there was some whispering and finger pointing. It all seemed relatively harmless and it did not appear as though anyone was going to alert the media.

Bobby and I were making small talk but I knew Bobby was really not there. We had placed our order when Bobby excused himself from the table. He pushed his chair back and as he stood up he explained he would be back in a minute. The minutes passed and I began to wonder what was taking so long. I realized that the men's room was in one direction and the bar was in the other direction. It occurred to me that Bobby had not walked in the direction of the men's room.

I got up from our table and walked into the bar area. Just as I had feared, Bobby was at the bar cupping a glass of whiskey and preparing himself for his first drink in nearly twelve years.

I walked up to Bobby and with a challenging tone in my voice, said "Hey! You're not really going to drink that, are you?"

Bobby said "I was thinking about it," adding, "What's the difference anyway? My life is over. My wife is dead. I am going to be railroaded for her murder. They have already tried me in the media and found me guilty. The Lottery Club Murderer."

Bobby drew the glass up to his lips and as he began to take a sip I threw my Hail Mary… "I have never known you to not stand up for what you know is right. Defend yourself. You're practically a lawyer for Christ's sake."

As Bobby laughed the whiskey sprayed from his mouth.

For the first time in days I saw the very start of a smile break across Bobby's face. He put the glass back down on the bar and said "You are right. I am going to stand up for what is right starting now!"

I had once again witnessed the flip of the switch. Bobby was again off and running, this time quite literally for his life. We both knew that if he was going to prove his innocence he would need one hell of a good attorney. We also knew that with his legal background and his vast knowledge of the law, Bobby would be his own best asset. If anyone could do this, it had to be Bobby.

Chapter Twelve

Bobby had originally wanted one of two prominent lawyers to take his case. Both had agreed to take the case if, and only if, they were given full control of the defense proceedings and would be allowed to delay the trial for several years. They felt this gave them the best chance at a positive outcome for Bobby. I agreed with this thought process wholeheartedly but Bobby was dead set against it. In the end both prominent lawyers refused to take the case because Bobby insisted on a speedy trial.

Finding a lawyer to defend Bobby proved to be no small task. Most lawyers wanted to extend the trial as long as possible. Only hours before the arraignment, Bobby was forced to use a lawyer that was less than 'prominent'. He was willing to do as Bobby instructed, but not without argument.

Bobby was arraigned the next morning and prior to the proceedings. The newly hired lawyer urged Bobby to allow him to do everything within his means to delay the trial as long as possible. Now that he was out on bail, they could easily stretch things out and postpone the trial for several years. The lawyer's argument was that by doing this, they would allow time for the media frenzy to die down.

Bobby was adamantly against this idea and was clear on the fact that there was no way he wanted this hanging over him any longer than was absolutely necessary. With that, Bobby instructed his lawyer to immediately invoke his right to a speedy trial. The judge seemed perturbed at Bobby's insistence and he assured both Bobby and his lawyer that he would not allow his courtroom to become a circus. He then promised everyone present that he would be fair but firm, that the law would prevail and that the court proceedings would be followed to the letter of the law. Both the defense and the prosecution were informed by the court that they had four months to prepare and the trial date was set.

Over the next four months, the evidence continued to pour in. Through the process of discovery, Bobby would soon learn the extent of the evidence that the prosecution had collected against him. The fact was that the evidence was mainly circumstantial, but the weight of it was certainly enough to cause concern. The investigation had concluded that a specific type of nut extract known as the chinkapin nut had been added to Dana's daily vitamins. A timeline had also been constructed and it clearly showed that Bobby had ample time to obtain the poison used. In addition to that, Bobby had access to the house and it was an undisputed fact that he had been in the house the night before the murder at Dana's request to collect his things. The EpiPen had also been found at the house next to Dana's body with the cap super-glued on. The type of glue used, however common it may have been, was the exact brand of glue that was in one of the kitchen drawers inside the house.

The bottom line was that although the evidence was circumstantial, it was certainly overwhelming. In spite of this, not only did Bobby have a certainty that he would he be found 'not guilty' and ultimately be acquitted of the murder charge in the courtroom, he was determined to prove his innocence as well.

Proving that Bobby had a motive may have been difficult if it hadn't been for the hundred plus women suing him for their share of the lottery money. The situation was so ridiculously convoluted that I am not sure how anyone would have known who it was necessary to kill to get the lottery money. Clearly, there was motive enough to go around.

More and more details were emerging from the computer the police had confiscated from Bobby's office. Less than twenty four hours before the murder, a search had been done on the computer that linked directly to the website of the Bavarian Nut Company in Clarence, NY. The search had been specifically for the chinkapin nut, which happened to also be the most deadly of the nuts that Dana was allergic to. The receptionist had given a statement that placed Bobby at the office at the approximate time the search had been done. I am sure it was nothing more than a poor choice of words on her part, but the statement she gave read that we had 'snuck in' through the back entrance. It almost seemed to suggest that Bobby had come specifically to use the computer for the search.

Most unsettling of all was that the Bavarian Nut Company in Clarence had been broken into some time after they had closed at 7pm the night before the murder.

The police report from that night indicated that there had been a break in through a window and the only thing taken had been a sampling of chinkapin nut extracts. This revelation, combined with the fact that Bobby's ez-pass proved that he had gotten off the thruway at 8:26 that evening just two blocks from the factory, was undoubtedly going to be tough to discount in the courtroom.

In addition, there was a four hour window of time between when Bobby had gotten off the thruway in Clarence until he checked into the hotel at 12:22am. Bobby would offer no explanation and no alibi for the time period. In hindsight, I don't understand what reason Bobby had for not telling the investigators that he had been at Elaine's house that night. There may have been a chance one of her neighbors had seen his car parked outside that night. Something like that could have possibly helped to exonerate him. I am his best friend and even I wouldn't find out where he had been that night until much later.

During the trial prep, the media never once let up. Bobby had been tried by the media before real trial had a chance to begin. The picture that had been painted of Bobby was that of a lying, manipulating, woman-izing murderer. I am not sure that Bobby's lawyer believed he was innocent. I have always believed in Bobby. No matter what, I had always known that when the chips were down I could always bet on him.

Life outside the courtroom continued to go on. The trial had become a huge financial burden and my father had insisted that Bobby not return to his job at the dealership until after he had been acquitted. I suspected that my father was not expecting that to ever happen. Instead, Bobby spent every minute outside the courtroom working on his own case and trying to find an answer to the question that had plagued him since the morning of the murder. Who had killed Dana?

There were times when Bobby would ask if I had heard from Elaine. I had not. I had driven out to her house once. It had been a day when I felt overwhelmingly sad at the realization I would probably never see her again. I wanted to see the house and maybe in some strange way I felt like I could find her there again. The day I was there, the landlord had been outside working and I stopped and introduced myself. He told me that he had not seen nor heard from her either. She had left the house, leaving almost everything but her clothes and a few personal possessions. She left behind a house full of furniture and high priced décor along with a check to cover the remainder of the lease. The landlord stated that he had thought the situation was very odd, but that he had lost nothing except a perfect tenant. We had both tried to reach her by phone only to learn that the cell number we had no longer worked.

I was certain that her leaving town had nothing to do with Bobby's troubles. She had written the letter to me the day before news of the murder. In my head I tried to tell myself that she was confused and still in pain over the death of her fiancé. Perhaps she had been developing feelings for me that frightened her. Or maybe I, in some way, reminded her of him. I had thought of at least a dozen reasons for her writing that letter. I missed her so much and hoped she was doing well, wherever she was. In my heart, I managed to keep a secret hope alive that she would suddenly realize that I had always been the one for her and she would come back to me. I fantasized scenarios in my imagination of her walking into the dealership on some random Tuesday afternoon. I wanted to kiss her and take her hand and take her home with me to stay. I knew that she felt that her fiancé had been the only "one". I believed that I was the "one", that everything that had ever happened to her had delivered her straight to me. She was meant to be with me, she just needed some time to get things straight in her head. It had to be. I hoped that someday we would be together again, and then we could finish what we started. Then we could finally have our happily ever after. I loved her so much.

This is what I told myself. It hurt too much to think any other way.

Life moved on and in the months leading up to the trial I heard nothing from Elaine. I went to work every day at the dealership and continued to support Bobby in every way I could.

Bobby was determined to clear his name and worked tirelessly on his own case. He knew the evidence against him inside and out. Less than a week before the trial was set to start, Bobby and I met at his attorney's office to do a mock trial together. I got to play Bobby and Bobby played the part of the District Attorney. Bobby's lawyer was, of course, the defense lawyer. As bizarre as it might seem, Bobby did a fantastic job of presenting the DA's case. This came as no surprise to any of us, yet it made me feel a little saddened to watch him present the case and see in him the lawyer he might have been. He presented the evidence in such a flawless and convincing way that I couldn't imagine the opposing attorney would be able to do any better. On the other hand, to my great disappointment, Bobby's attorney seemed to be stumbling and was in no way instilling confidence in either Bobby or myself. During the course of our practice session, there were several times that

Bobby would say something that should have produced an objection from the defense table, but none came. After Bobby spoke, he gave his attorney time to react. Sometimes it took a fifteen to twenty second stare before the lawyer would push his chair back and jump to his feet with the expected "Objection, Your Honor!" Even then the lawyer seemed startled and somewhat unsure of himself as he explained the reason for his objection. Bobby then turned in my direction and with a half joking and half serious tone he said, "I'm going to fucking prison, aren't I?"

I admit that I was scared, but I saw no reason for Bobby to know. Instead, I shrugged his question off with a laugh and assured him that there was no way that the DA would ever be able to present the case as well or as convincingly as Bobby had in practice. I also knew that Bobby would be sitting at the table with his attorney throughout the proceedings. I knew that Bobby would be there to nudge his attorney along. Bobby agreed completely and told me that he had every intention of doing as much as he could as far as presenting the case and cross-examining witnesses. "If I didn't need to have a license to practice law, I wouldn't even have that guy in the courtroom with me!" He told me as we left the office later that evening.

Chapter Thirteen

Jury selection began on a Monday morning in mid-January. The tension in the courtroom that day was almost unbearable. Dana's parents were there, along with other friends and family members. They all seemed intent on making sure Bobby paid for the crime they were convinced he had committed.

The attorneys barely argued during the jury selection process. Bobby's lawyer had advised him that he wanted to get as many men as possible on the jury for obvious reasons. Bobby seemed to have his own opinion on the balance of men and women in his jury and in the end, there were eight women and only four men.

His lawyer stated, for the record, that he thought this was a mistake on Bobby's part. I admit that I also believed that Bobby had made a mistake. Bobby disagreed and seemed as calm and cool as ever. He confidently explained to us that he felt it would help him more than it would hurt to have more women on the jury. He added that he thought that the decision should be his considering it was his life that was on the line.

Bobby's confidence and borderline cockiness were more than a little unsettling to me. I had a tough time believing that he could effectively charm these women out of a murder charge from the defendant's seat at his own trial. I thought to myself that Bobby was either a genius or he had completely lost his mind. By the end of the trial we would certainly find out which was the case.

The jury was seated in less than two days and the trial was set begin the following day at 9:30. That day began with the usual opening statements from each side. The DA assured everyone in the courtroom that he would prove beyond a shadow of a doubt that Bobby had, with malice and intent, murdered his wife and that he should be convicted of the first degree murder charge.

Bobby's defense attorney gave a reasonably confident opening statement whereby he suggested that the State's case against Bobby was purely circumstantial and based very little in fact.

The DA's case was indeed circumstantial, but the weight of the evidence against Bobby was undeniable. They had created visual aids in the DA's office to help present their case which all seemed to impress the jurors. There was a timeline that, in actuality, proved nothing more than the fact that Bobby's computer had been used to search for chinkapin nuts and that he had no alibi from 6:30pm the night before until the morning of the murder. The three minute conversation with the hotel desk clerk wasn't enough to help in any way.

By the time the DA had finished presenting his case, there was no doubt in any of our minds that he had painted an extremely dark picture of Bobby. Against opposition by the defense attorney, the judge had overruled his objection and allowed Bobby's prior felony to be admitted into evidence. This opened the door for the DA to mention Bobby's father's attempted murder conviction. Although the immediate objection made by Bobby's lawyer was sustained and the jury consequently instructed to disregard what they had heard, the damage had been done. As they say, you can't un-ring a bell. The jury now knew about Bobby's past as well as that of his father. I stared silently at Bobby. I knew him better than anyone and although he wasn't showing it, I knew the anger was building up inside him as his mind absorbed the words of the DA's assault on his character.

As anticipated, the DA had indeed painted a gruesomely vivid picture of Bobby as a felon, a womanizer and an adulterer. He described Bobby as having a self-centered, self-serving, egotistical personality beyond redemption. He then stated that it wasn't out of the question or at all far-fetched to imagine that Bobby had graduated to murder. After all, what wouldn't Bobby be willing to do if it served his purposes?

Admittedly, the DA was not far from the truth where most of his statement was concerned, but Bobby was not a murderer. Facts were facts and at some level, the DA was pretty much on target with what he had said about Bobby. Things were not looking good for

Bobby's case. With that statement officially in the court record, the prosecution rested its case.

I breathed a deep breath with the realization that it was time to present Bobby's defense. From the beginning, it had been the strategy of both Bobby and his lawyer to systematically, piece by piece, dispose of the evidence that had been presented. The evidence that was the basis of the prosecution's case was not only circumstantial, it also lacked any real substance. That, combined with the fact that there was no actual physical evidence that Bobby had killed Dana, was the foundation of Bobby's defense. We all wondered what would happen as it was still unclear as to whether Bobby would actually take the stand in his own defense or not.

We all knew this was a no win situation for Bobby. If he did not take the stand, we were afraid it would appear as though he was guilty and was trying to hide something. If he agreed to take the stand, the DA would most assuredly bring up all of the affairs and every detail he could manage to get in about The Lottery Club. There was no doubt that all of this would only serve to further hurt Bobby's character and, more importantly, his likability in the juror's eyes.

After great consideration by Bobby and against the recommendation of his lawyer, Bobby decided it was more important to him that the jury hear in his own words that he was not responsible for Dana's death. Knowing Bobby as I do, I think it was as important to him that he went on record stating that he did not kill Dana as it was for him to tell the jury.

There was a part of me that thought this may be Bobby's undoing. I also believed that if anyone could make the jury like him, it was Bobby himself. It had been ten days since the trial had started and with eight days of testimony presenting the DA's case, Friday had ended with the prosecution resting its case. With that, the stage was set for the defense to begin presenting its case on Monday morning.

On our way out of the courthouse that afternoon, I asked Bobby for his opinion on the DA's case. For the first time ever I think I saw fear in Bobby's eyes, or perhaps it was rage. Bobby was furious that they had been allowed to bring in any information about his father or about Bobby's previous conviction before he had even had the opportunity to take the stand in his own defense.

If there had been any question before, it was now crystal clear to Bobby that it was an imperative that he take the stand. At 9am Monday morning it would be the defense's turn to change the tide and undo the damage done by the DA. Somehow, there had to be a way to plant reasonable doubt in the minds of the twelve people now in charge of Bobby's future. Bobby and the lawyer had several heated discussions about how the case should be presented. Bobby wanted to use the fact that the housekeeper had access and knowledge of their home, not to mention full knowledge of Dana's allergies and the location of her EpiPen. Maggie, the housekeeper, was also a member of The Lottery Club. Bobby insisted that the woman had no alibi for that night either and Bobby was prepared to suggest that it was she that had poisoned the vitamins. His instincts and a vast personal knowledge of Maggie led him to believe that she was the killer. She had a history of mild violence against past boyfriends. Bobby was privy to information that she had even put a large dose of Visine in a man's drink once that sent him to the hospital with a violent stomach reaction. This could never be proven, but she had told Bobby all about it during one of their several sexual encounters. Although it was not unlike the expectations of the other women in the club, Maggie had asked Bobby one time, "If something bad happened to your wife, will we be together?"

It was a question he had been asked numerous times, yet he insisted that there had been something different in the way she had asked and the look in her eyes as she had asked the question.

It was soon after that conversation that Bobby had ended their sexual involvement. Although Maggie had never said anything to Dana, her attitude was markedly different from that day forward. The house was never again as tidy as it had been in the past. It always seemed that there was something she had forgotten to do, or just hadn't been able to get to. It also seemed more and more like things that were important to Dana had ended up broken. Bobby desperately wanted to put the woman on the stand and question her about Dana's murder and her whereabouts that night.

In the end, his attorney advised Bobby that it would be a mistake and explained that the whole sordid story would make him look really bad in the eyes of the jurors, especially the females. Eventually, Bobby agreed that it may not be the best thing to do, that the jury might feel as though he was bullying her and unjustly accusing her of the crime he was himself on trial for.

We worked together the entire weekend preparing for the presentation of Bobby's defense. We pulled together our plan to discredit the DA's case and then finish with Bobby's testimony. We realized that Bobby's answers had to convince the jury that he was telling the truth as well as change the jury's perception of Bobby as presented by the prosecution. While it looked as though we would be able to present a relatively strong defense by showing that the DA's case was primarily based on circumstantial evidence and without substance, Bobby was still fixated on discovering the real killer.

Sunday night, Bobby wanted to be alone to have time to go over, in his head, every possible question he thought the prosecutor might ask on cross examination. He insisted to both me and his lawyer that he had every intention of answering every question truthfully. He was certain that it would make it easier to answer every question without hesitation and would therefore make him seem more believable.

Bobby had been alone in his hotel room for more than an hour when he heard a knock on the door. When Bobby answered the door, the female detective, Kelly, was in the hall. Bobby was puzzled as to why she had come to the hotel.

"The trial started two weeks ago, you can't question me anymore." He explained as he stood in the doorway to his room.

She assured him that she was not there on official police business and asked if she could come in the room to speak with him.

"Of course," Bobby said as he took a step back from the door and motioned her into his room. "What's on your mind?"

The information that she had for Bobby that night would change the entire nature of the case from that day forward. She began by asking Bobby to promise that he would never reveal her as the source of the information she was about to give him.

"You have my word." Bobby promised and she began by telling him what he already knew.

"The DA has it in for you in a big way, Bobby. He seems to think he can build his career on this case. Also, the judge's niece is one of the women in The Lottery Club."

She went on for almost an hour explaining details that Bobby had not been aware of. She had concerns other than the judge's questionable decision to continue to hear the case in his courtroom in spite of his relationship to one of the women in the club. It was one detail that had been left out of the press and on its own was more of a moral problem than a legal issue. In addition to that, she explained that there had been some potentially important evidence that had been covered up by the judge and one of the detectives on the case. It was evidence that might have shed light on other possible suspects, but it was determined to have had nothing to do with the case.

Apparently, there had been a few blonde hairs found at the house the day of the murder. They had been stuck on the sliding door on the back of the house. There had also been a very tiny smudge of rose colored lipstick found on the door casing. It seemed to the detective as though someone had managed somehow to squeeze him or herself out the door.

Bobby immediately remembered that when he had been in the house the night before the murder, the sliding door had been stuck open maybe nine or ten inches. He told the detective the story and it seemed to fit that whoever had been in the house to poison the vitamins that night had heard Bobby come into the house to collect his personal belongings. The door had a tendency to become stuck just less than a foot open to the point where it could neither be opened all the way nor could it be closed easily. This information seemed to coincide almost too perfectly with Bobby's theory that Maggie had been the murderer. She had blonde hair, wore what Bobby considered to be that shade of lipstick and most importantly, she had a motive.

Needless to say, Bobby was stunned with what he had learned. He was still unsure of what to do with what he knew, but somehow it breathed new life into his theory on the murder.

He sat quietly and thought for a few minutes before thanking Kelly and asked if there was anything else that he should know. Kelly nodded her head.

"The very same lipstick and hair was found in the window frame that night at the nut factory."

Bobby was excited and at the same time speechless. It was beyond comprehension why anyone would have kept evidence like that covered up. The break-in at the nut factory happened the very night that Bobby suspected someone of having been in the house for the purpose of poisoning Dana.

The detective apologized again for not having come forward sooner with the information. Bobby understood that she had a valid reason for being scared and assured her that he was grateful she had taken the time to come to the hotel and talk with him.

Bobby showed the detective out of the room and as he closed the door and sat on the edge of the bed in his room, he began to consider what he would do with what he now knew. First and foremost, he wanted to make the judge aware that he knew about the hair and the lipstick at both crime scenes. Perhaps this knowledge could save him from having to take the stand the next morning as the prosecution's final witness in their case.

That night Bobby slept well with the knowledge that all he needed to do was have DNA testing done on the hair and lipstick samples and link them to Maggie. His trial would end tomorrow and not only would he be free, he would be able to prove who it was that really had killed Dana. It was the best news Bobby had heard in a very long time.

Bobby arrived early at his attorney's office the next morning. He explained that the detective and been to see him and shared the information he had learned the night before. The attorney immediately made a call to the courthouse and requested a meeting with the judge before court was in session again that morning. They set a time to meet in chambers and although they had hoped it could be done without the prosecution present, the DA was already inside when Bobby and his lawyer arrived.

Inside the judge's chambers, Bobby's attorney began spewing legal jargon and an impatient Bobby interrupted him mid-sentence and immediately cut to the chase himself.

"I know all about the evidence," he began as the judge and DA looked on, unsure of what Bobby thought he knew. "I know about the hair and the lipstick."

Bobby insisted that at the very least, the evidence be admitted into court and demanded that the judge reopen the investigation. The defense was prepared to argue that it was grounds for a mistrial.

"I don't have blonde hair and I sure as hell don't wear lipstick!" Bobby shouted. The judge was dumbfounded as to how this information had been leaked to Bobby, but in an extremely stern manner informed Bobby again that he had no intention of letting the trial become a circus. "I made the decision to keep the press out of my courtroom," he admonished Bobby and continued, "There are no members of your little club allowed in the courtroom because it was my decision to keep this trial from becoming out of control."

What the judge would say next crushed Bobby's hopes of ending his nightmare.

"I have been aware of the evidence for months. The state immediately had the hair and the lipstick tested against every single member of The Lottery Club. Including the young lady you are so determined to implicate as the killer. Each and every member tested negatively as a match. It was my decision that it was not necessary information for the defense to have."

The DA quickly added, "That is something you can take up on appeal if necessary."

Bobby was deflated. His lawyer calmly leaned toward him and whispered "Let's just finish this. We have a good defense prepared and if the worst case scenario happens, we now have solid grounds for an appeal. Who knows, perhaps we can use it to argue for a mistrial. This is far from over and you know it."

He looked at the clock on the desk and it was already five minutes to nine. The defense was more than prepared to present its case as soon as court was called into session but Bobby continued to sit motionless in the chair, stunned and dazed at what had just happened. He silently questioned himself as to how his instincts could have been so wrong. He attempted to rationalize it all by telling himself that the DNA tests had to have been wrong. The only thing that made any sense to Bobby was that the killer was one of the women in the club.

Chapter Fourteen

We walked into the courtroom together before the jury was brought in for the morning. I sat in my usual spot behind the defense table and put my hand on Bobby's shoulder for reassurance as we waited for the judge to walk in and take his seat at the bench. When Bobby turned in his seat to look at me, I could tell that his mind was reeling. The DA had come in for the day with an especially confident demeanor, bordering on cocky. It was funny how he suddenly reminded me so much of Bobby. I think he truly believed that he would be able to bully and embarrass Bobby on the stand if he was given the opportunity. I was sure he would try, but I knew he would have his hands full when it came to questioning Bobby.

Bobby adjusted the suit jacket he had worn that day and picked up the small glass of water on the defense table in front of him to take a drink. He sat the glass back down and in the silence of the courtroom he quickly surveyed the people that were there in the courtroom that day. His eyes stopped as he noticed a familiar face only two rows from the back. "How did she get in?" He whispered without expecting an answer.

Katie smiled at Bobby as his eyes locked on her. Puzzled as to how she had gotten inside, Bobby decided she must have lied or somehow convinced the bailiff to let her in. Just then, the door of the judge's chambers opened and Bobby's attention was back on the trial.

A moment later I was again witnessing the flip of a switch in Bobby's mind as he turned and started giving instructions to his lawyer. Of course, no one could hear what was being said but it was obvious to me that the lawyer was dead-set against whatever it was that Bobby was proposing to do. Clearly, Bobby had a plan in his head and we were all about to find out what it was. When Bobby leaned back in his chair, I could read the words on his lips as he said to his lawyer, "I got it covered."

The judge tapped the gavel bringing the court into session for the morning as he asked, "Is the defense ready to present its case?"

Hesitantly, Bobby's lawyer pushed his chair back and stood up to answer and then quickly sat back in his seat. "We are, Your Honor."

"Please proceed," the judge instructed.

Without hesitation, Bobby's lawyer was back on his feet again, this time with a confidence that hadn't shown moments earlier when the judge had asked if he was prepared to begin his case.

"The defense calls Mr. Robert Ferrari to the stand."

Both the judge and the DA were noticeably stunned. The courtroom became loud with a hundred little gasps and whispers as Bobby stood and took the stand. Another minute later, silence had returned and everyone's focus was on Bobby.

My immediate thought was that Bobby had completely lost his mind. I couldn't begin to imagine what he was thinking in that moment. I thought to myself that maybe Bobby was beginning to let his anger and frustration get the better of him. I silently willed my friend to pull himself together.

Bobby was sworn in and his lawyer began. "Please state your name."

"Robert Ferrari."

"Your witness…" Bobby's lawyer said as he turned to look at the DA.

Almost simultaneously, both the DA and the judge responded. "I beg your pardon?"

"YOUR WITNESS, SIR" he repeated in an irritated tone as he walked back to his seat at the table.

It was clear to me that if it had been Bobby's intention to catch everyone off guard, he had certainly succeeded. The DA began shuffling papers and searching through his notes.

Speaking in the direction of the prosecution, the judge did not wait long before ordering the lawyer to "Please proceed."

"Yes, Your Honor" he responded as he put a folder full of papers back down on the table and approached Bobby.

"Well, Mr. Ferrari, I had been wondering if you were planning to take the stand."

"Of course. Why wouldn't I?" Bobby smirked tauntingly at the man standing in front of him.

"I would really hope that this isn't some elaborate game you have planned to try to prove your innocence." The DA snarled back at Bobby.

Bobby calmly looked across the courtroom as he thought and then answered, "You know very well that it is not up to me to 'prove my innocence'. It has always been my understanding that in a criminal court I am presumed innocent until proven guilty."

A few chuckles came from the seats behind me and I felt myself smile at Bobby. It seemed that Bobby was indeed in control, at least for the moment.

The DA took one deep breath and wasted no time in getting to work on Bobby. He asked if Bobby was aware that the civil case against him had concluded the previous Friday afternoon. For the record, the DA stated that the judge in that case had divided the $105 million lottery jackpot in the following manner. Each of the one hundred one women named in the lawsuit against Bobby had received one million dollars. The judge then set aside the remaining four million to be awarded to Dana's family if they prevailed in their separate civil case against Bobby.

"Clearly I am aware of those facts. It has been the lead story on every local and national news for the past 48 hours. Not only am I aware of it, I am positive that everyone in this courtroom is aware of it. Quite possibly everyone in the country is aware of it."

The giggles spread across the courtroom as Bobby answered the DA's question.

The DA was not impressed with Bobby's candor and didn't wait for the courtroom to become quiet again.

"Of the hundred one women, Mr. Ferrari, let's say plus or minus five- how many of them were you intimate with?" he asked in a way that almost begged Bobby to respond that he had been with every one of the women.

Bobby smiled back at the lawyer and very coolly stated, "None of them."

The chorus of "ooooo"'s filled the courtroom followed by an immediate hush as everyone waited for what was next.

"What exactly do you mean by that?"

Bobby's tone made it sound as if he was reprimanding the DA for overstepping his bounds and he began to answer the question.

"I think the question you meant to ask me was, 'how many of the women did I have sex with?'"

Again, the sound of quiet giggles filled the courtroom as Bobby answered his own question, "Sixty-five. Plus or minus five."

The laughter exploded through the room as the judge slammed the gavel down and ordered silence. The DA smiled at Bobby and nodded as if in agreement. He glared at Bobby for a second or two as if to let Bobby know that he had no intention of letting Bobby steal the show and get the better of him.

The DA stepped back, looked at the floor and then the ceiling as he took a deep breath and said, "Of the sixty five plus women you admit to having sex with, how many of them did you love?"

Bobby hesitated for a moment as he waited to hear the objection from the side of the courtroom where his lawyer sat. He was as totally captivated by the scene as the rest of us. We all sensed the animosity that was building and Bobby corrected the man before answering the question, "Sixty Five. Plus OR MINUS. And to answer your question- all of them."

I could hear the people behind me whispering back and forth between each other. The DA immediately asked again, "Let me repeat the question. How many of the women that you have had sex with were you in love with?"

In an increasingly loud and annoyed tone, Bobby did not hesitate with his answer, "None of them. You are asking a different question. I loved each and every one of them. I was 'in love' with none of them."

The sound of the gavel again brought the courtroom to attention and the DA continued. "Touche. Mr. Ferrari. Let's see if you can have as much fun with my next question."

Everyone in the courtroom could feel the tension. My heart was about to beat out of my chest as we all waited. We waited not so much for the next question, but we waited in great anticipation of how Bobby would answer that question.

"Mr. Ferrari, I'll ask the exact question I want you to answer this time." It felt as though everyone was holding their breath as the question was asked, "Mr. Ferrari, were you in love with your wife?"

Bobby's eyes flashed at his attorney as if waiting to be rescued by the sound of "Your Honor, I object. Irrelevant." The objection never came. The seconds ticked away seemingly like hours as Bobby briefly hesitated. He knew that the longer he waited, the worse he would look in the eyes of the jurors. He looked at the DA and then toward the jury as he slowly began his answer with a confidence that belied the anxiety I knew my friend must have felt in that moment.

"I will answer the question. It is an exceptionally complicated answer." He looked again at the DA and asked, "Can I have your assurance that you will allow me the time to give my complete answer without interruption?"

"You have my word," the DA promised as he motioned to Bobby as if to say, 'the floor is yours'.

Neither I nor anyone else in the room had the slightest idea of what Bobby was about to say. I could tell from the light in Bobby's eyes that it was something profound. As Bobby hesitated for a moment and then stood up, I knew that what would follow would be extraordinary.

"Thank you," Bobby began, "Mr. Di'Atteti, you asked me about intimacy when you meant to ask about sex. The two words have nothing to do with each other. I have only been intimate with two women in my entire life. One was a young woman that I loved many years ago. I shared my deepest secrets, hopes, dreams and fears with her. She shared the same with me. She was the one that was truly there for me when my mom died. We shared a closeness that I had never felt with anyone before and with only one woman since. I was in love with her at the time and I will always love her for that."

I knew immediately that he was talking about Penny, but I was riveted on every word he was saying.

He continued, "There came a time when that young woman broke my heart. I didn't realize at the time the effect that the end of that relationship would have on my life. I could have never imagined that the scars left by a sixteen year old would be so deep. I buried the feelings of betrayal and I think that I subconsciously built a wall to protect myself from ever feeling hurt like that again. Between the death of my mom and the betrayal of my first love, my heart was damaged and I became the person I am today. A person capable of creating something as outrageous and incredible as The Lottery Club.

From then on, it was never about intimacy, or love for that matter. It was about sex and having fun. It was about personal pleasures and it was mainly about avoiding intimacy. I understand that some of you may be horrified to hear someone admit these things. I assure you that I was not the only guilty party in the arrangements I had with women. With very few exceptions, each and every woman I was ever with had their own agenda and rarely was it 'love'. In high school it was all about being with the popular guy with the nice car. In college they all wanted the star soccer player with the bright promising future as a lawyer.

After college, the women I was with wanted the charming, sweet- talking Bobby. I gave them all exactly what they wanted. They got no more and no less. It was always about what they wanted. The Lottery Club started the same way. It was always about what the women wanted from me. They got exactly what they gave. I regret nothing. They all knew the deal going in. Without exception, they all knew I was married. They all knew I was never going to leave my wife. They had a dream of a life that never existed and that they knew was never possible. I am sorry if anyone felt hurt. It was never my intention to do anything but have fun. We were all adults. We were all willing participants in a game that was allowed to get completely out of hand. I never intended any of this. The Lottery Club grew and it was impossible to deny the fun I was having.

It was only a few years ago that I met an honest, beautiful person that walked into my work one day to buy a car. From the moment I saw her, I wanted her in the club. From the moment she said her first words to me, I knew that was not a possibility. She came to me and we talked. I recognized the pain the moment I really saw her. She told me with tears in her eyes about the death of her fiancé. She shared her fears and her secrets with me. She talked about how her hopes for the life she envisioned with him had been crushed in an instant. Without any agenda, she became a true friend that I loved. She took one look at the walls that surrounded my soul and without a second thought for herself, she walked through. It is only now at this very moment as I tell you this that I realize that I am in love with her as well."

I literally heard the tell-tale sniffling of crying women behind me as Bobby took another deep breath and continued.

"Doesn't matter anyway. She is gone now. And to answer the question that must be on at least a few of your minds at this point, no. No. I did not have sex with her, but we were intimate with each other on levels that I doubt most of you can even begin to comprehend."

Bobby then turned his eyes toward me as if to say he was sorry. I smiled back to reassure my friend that I understood and loved him anyway.

"You asked the question, was I in love with my wife? I tell you truthfully, yes. Yes, I loved my wife. In whatever capacity I was able to be in love with someone, I was in love with her. I really had no understanding of how to be intimate with her. I was not and I failed as a husband in that respect as well as many others. I regret that and I wish she were here today to hear my apology. I would want her to know that it was not her fault and that I loved her.

The fact of the matter is this, I was in love with my wife. I was in love with her in the only way I was able to be in love.

Furthermore, I will answer the next question you are about to ask me, Mr. Di'Atteti."

Bobby's eyes were welling up with tears. A couple of the jurors were holding tissues. The women behind me, and I suspect even a couple of men, continued to sniffle.

"You can be one hundred percent certain that I did not kill my wife. I will find out who is responsible and I will see that justice is served," Bobby repeated, "I did not kill my wife," as he fell back into his seat.

We all sat motionless in our seats. Even the DA seemed at a loss for words. Bobby was suddenly a real human being to everyone in the courtroom that day. The members of the jury, who had never known anything of Bobby before the beginning of the trial, seemed to soften as they listened to Bobby speak. He became a real person just like the rest of us. The pain he felt was undeniable. It remained unclear to me whether or not this had been something that would ultimately help his case. One unmistakable fact remained, I had been Bobby's friend for forty years and I finally felt that day as though I was finally able to understand what it was that made Bobby "Bobby".

The silence inside the court continued for what seemed like hours. The DA himself was taking longer than he should have to regain his composure. Eventually, there were the sounds of people moving around in their seats and the DA walked back to his table to pick up some notes he had written on a pad of paper. He read through the first page and as he flipped to the next, he looked up at Bobby and resumed his attack.

"Mr. Ferrari, thank you for your little trip down memory lane and the interpretation of love and intimacy as seen through the eyes of Bobby Ferrari. As I look through the hundred and one signed Lottery Club contracts and the one hundred and one court petitions signed against you in civil court, I realize that what I feel most for you is pity. Your inability to love someone and share any level of intimacy with anyone is clear to all of us. I think we can be sure that to the same extent you were unable to love any of the women in the club; they too were unable to love you. Perhaps if things had been different and one of these women had truly loved you, she would have not pursued a case against you in civil court. The fact remains that every one of these women wanted the money more than they ever wanted you. Perhaps if one of the women had loved you, she might have been willing to kill your wife for you. You have insisted from the beginning that it was a member of your club that murdered your wife. I have to agree with you there, Mr. Ferrari, but it wasn't one of the hundred and one names on The Lottery Club contracts or one of the hundred and one names in your computer that murdered your wife. It was the original member of The Lottery Club, Mr. Ferrari, it was you that killed your wife. You know the truth and I believe that the jury now knows it as well."

The courtroom had fallen silent yet again and the only thing I could hear was my own breathing. There was a long pause before the DA again began to speak.

Bobby interrupted him, "Pardon me, you mean one hundred two members of The Lottery Club, do you not? Mr. Di'Atteti?"

Apparently, something the DA had said triggered something in Bobby's head and I saw a glimmer of hope in Bobby's face.

"No, Mr Ferrari, I meant that there were one hundred one names on the computer print out."

Bobby wasn't even listening to what the DA was saying and in an almost surreal fashion, Bobby almost screamed "I know who killed my wife and I can prove it!"

The court erupted in a series of gasps and whispers as the judge again admonished everyone present with the promise that he would clear the courtroom if there were another outburst.

Bobby's lawyer pushed his chair back and jumped up, immediately asking the judge if he could approach the bench. He had no idea what- or who- Bobby was referring to and wanted to stop Bobby from blurting out something in court that could potentially hurt their case.

In front of the judge, Bobby pleaded for two minutes in front of his computer to find the evidence he needed to prove that not only did he have nothing to do with Dana's death, but that he knew the identity of the person that did. He had already added up the evidence in his own mind and was certain that they could match the woman with the hair and lipstick found at both the scene of the crime as well as the nut factory.

While both the judge and the DA were in agreement that this was an unusual request, they were willing to give Bobby the time he asked for.

The judge addressed the jury and informed them that they were to be removed from the courtroom. Silence reigned over the court as we all waited as Bobby whispered to his attorney who in turn whispered to the court bailiff. The bailiff nodded in response as they began to boot up the computer. Everything appeared to move in slow motion as we waited. Bobby stood in front of the computer with the attorneys and the judge looking on. From the table next to the computer, he picked up the timeline the prosecution had provided.

"Please pay attention. This is extremely important." Bobby began, "The timeline shows that at 3:14 pm on September 11th, someone logged onto my computer to research where they could find chinkapin nuts in the Buffalo area."

The prosecution had used the fact that the search had been done on Bobby's computer as evidence that he had committed the crime. Bobby turned from his computer and asked the judge, "What is today's date?"

"Today is January 20th." The judge responded in a very matter-of –fact manner.

"Look at the date on the computer." Bobby stepped back as the group of men all moved closer to look at the computer screen. Clearly, the date on the bottom right hand side of the screen read "1/21"

The judge stated that he did not understand what Bobby was getting at and warned him against any more distractions. The DA just stood there trying to comprehend the point that Bobby was trying to make.

"My computer has always been a day ahead for no apparent reason. Whoever it was that logged onto my computer that day is the same person that killed Dana." Bobby continued with his theory, "Whoever was on my computer logged on the day BEFORE news broke that I had won the lottery. I wasn't even in town the day the computer search was done. I believe your timeline clearly shows that."

Bobby said to the DA, "Thank you for stating what I had been missing all along. There were two members of the original lottery club. When you said that the murderer was the original member, you were exactly correct."

Bobby then explained to the DA that the only person with both access and a reason to log onto his computer that day was the other original member, Katie.

From the back of the room where she had sat silently with the rest of us came Katie's distressed cry, "Bobby! What are you talking about? I love you and I always have. That is why I didn't sue for the money like all the others did. It was never about the money Bobby. I wanted you."

Without hesitation, the judge ordered the bailiff to arrest Katie for the murder of Dana Ferrari. He requested that a DNA test be performed immediately on the hair and lipstick.

Bobby explained the situation to the judge with regard to why there had been no contract with Katie. Since she had been the original member of The Lottery Club there had been no contract for her to sign. Bobby began asking members to sign contracts after he had conceived the idea in his head the day that Katie and he had initially discussed the lottery. As to why her name was not on the computer, Bobby was unable to provide a good explanation other than suggesting that she had deleted her information from the program the very same day she had logged the cars into his computer and performed the search for chinkapin nuts. Bobby wasn't sure of how she had gotten access to his program. It was hard to imagine that she had somehow guessed his password. It was more likely that in his excitement to leave town to pick up his Dodge Challenger that he had inadvertently left the program open on his computer. Still in shock and trying to put the details together himself, Bobby had developed a theory. He suggested that Katie had gone in to log the cars into his computer while he was out of town, noticed the program for the club open on his computer and discovered that Bobby was doing the same thing with all the other women and she became angry. Bobby surmised that in a jealous rage, she decided to frame Bobby for the murder of his own wife. Interestingly enough as it turned out, the murder had nothing to do with the actual lottery win. It had been the actions of a jealous woman and the motive all along had not been money, but love.

Bobby turned from the computer to address the DA who was now standing directly to Bobby's right. "Thank you, again, Mr. Di'Atteti for pointing out that the motive was love." He said as if to suggest that the DA had been the one to finally solve the case and exonerate him.

Without further delay, the judge suspended the trial pending the results of the tests. Weeks later, results of the testing were conclusive. The blonde hair found in the door casing and the window frame matched Katie.

Chapter Fifteen

By now it had been over five and a half months since Dana's death and Bobby's ordeal was almost over. The charges against him had been dropped and the media attention was diminishing. Bobby was wrapping up his civil court appearances and had asked me to attend the last day of the wrongful death suit filed against him by Dana's family. The outcome was exactly as we had anticipated. Dana's family was awarded the remaining $4 million from the lottery as well as the house they had shared.

While the news crews were present that day for the follow up to the big story, the big news that week was that the owner of the second lottery ticket had never come forward for their share of the jackpot. The ticket had been purchased in Pennsylvania and was due to expire in less than two weeks.

We walked out of the courtroom together that day and as we did, it occurred to me that my friend was just about broke. Although the charges against him had been dropped, his reputation had been destroyed. He could not come back to work at the dealership for obvious reasons. I had pulled together some money to give to Bobby that day. I knew that with all of the loose ends tied up, he was anxious to leave town and get a fresh start somewhere else. As we approached the door to leave the building, Bobby put his arm around me and we shared a quick hug as he thanked me.

"What are you going to do now?" I asked my friend, fully expecting a smile and a wink along with his now trademark response that he had it 'covered'.

Instead, Bobby appeared very thoughtful as he admitted, "To be honest with you, I'm not really sure. Before any of this happened, you asked me what I would do if I won and I told you 'Don't worry, I got it covered.' The truth is, I can't honestly tell you. I don't know if I have it covered or not. I have maybe $20,000 left and I think I will move to Arizona. I will get a job and try to build a life for myself. I promise no more lottery clubs."

We shared a laugh and hugged again.

"Let me know where you are when you get there and if you need anything, let me know."

With his impeccable timing and ability to seize the right moment, Bobby assured me with a smile.

"Don't worry, I got it covered."

We left together and walked down the steps of the courthouse. As we walked and talked about something totally unimportant I saw a look come over his face. It was a look I hadn't seen in quite some time. It was a look of surprise, shock and happiness all at the same moment. It was the same kind of happiness he had about him the day we had left to go to Pennsylvania on our ill-fated trip to buy his dream car.

As I turned to look at what it was that had suddenly grabbed Bobby's attention, I saw it. "Would you look at that," I said as we both stopped walking and stood staring at the immaculate black 1973 Dodge Challenger at the bottom of the courthouse steps. I said, "What are the chances…" and as I turned and saw the devilish grin on Bobby's face, I stopped mid-sentence.

Bobby just smiled and said, "Maybe I really do have it covered. It looks like we are about to find out."

We began to walk again slowly down the steps toward the car. Almost as if by magic, the beautiful Elaine suddenly stepped out of the driver's seat and looked over the roof of the car at both Bobby and me. My heart began to pound at the sight of the woman I loved and she smiled at me for what seemed like an eternity. In actuality, it was probably more like a mere second before she turned her focus to Bobby. She was waving a note in one hand that said, "You're the only one I can trust with this. Love, Bobby." In her other hand, she was holding the yet unclaimed lottery ticket.

A beaming smile came over her face as she said, "I think we have a date at the lottery office."

Suddenly, pieces began falling into place and I understood why Bobby had insisted on the stop at the post office the day he won the lottery. For a moment, I felt even more heartbroken at the thought that this may have been the reason for the letter she wrote to me. It took only a second after I had the thought for me to realize that the letter had been left at my office the day before the news that Bobby had won the lottery. Obviously, one had nothing to do with the other. Reality again set in and I knew in my heart that Elaine had ended things based solely on the fact that she wasn't able to love me the way I loved her. The letter had been painfully clear on that fact.

In the end, it really didn't matter. My heart was broken and my mind had set to work on rationalizing why it had happened the way it had. Perhaps she had realized that it was Bobby that she loved and had finally admitted it to herself. Bobby had come to the same conclusion in the courtroom during the murder trial only weeks before.

The irrefutable fact was that in spite of my personal misery, I was truly happy for the two people I loved and cared so much for. For them, I saw the potential for an amazing life together and a chance at a kind of love that continued to elude me. I knew in my heart that after what they had both been through, they deserved the exceptional future they were destined to share.

Independently of each other, I had heard each of them talk about traveling the world and their individual desires to do great things in other people's lives. Now they had each other and they had the means by which to accomplish their dreams. It seemed almost too perfect and, in a way, even I could not deny the magic the universe had seemingly performed in their lives. Their life together was poised to begin in that very moment and all I had to do was stand back and watch. I silently wished for them a life full of the happiness and love. I smiled inside and out as I watched my friend run to Elaine.

For the first time, Bobby kissed Elaine passionately on the lips. He stopped for a moment and held her face in his hands as he said "I love you."

Elaine smiled back at Bobby with a smile that lit up her eyes and said, "I know. I love you, too."

It looked like a scene from a movie screen as I waited and watched. I looked around and noticed other people noticing the scene as well. It is nearly impossible to put a name on the emotion I was feeling as I watched them together. It was overwhelming to me the moment Bobby suddenly became aware of himself again as he looked at me and ran back to where we been standing together only moments before.

He hugged me like he had never hugged me before and I knew my friend had found a happiness he had never imagined. He quietly said "I'm sorry."

I stepped back away from him and looked him straight in the eye and informed him that he had absolutely nothing to apologize for.

"I always knew you were destined for greatness. Now go do awesome things and don't disappoint me!" I said with a smile.

Bobby said that it was his initial plan to take Elaine away on a vacation. He wanted time alone with her in a way that he had not yet been able to enjoy. He also wanted relaxing time with her to brainstorm ideas on where they planned to start in terms of their dreams of helping people- and the world as a whole.

"Hey, why don't you come with us?" Bobby asked in a flash of excitement.

"No. I really have things to do at the dealership. I have things to catch up on after all the time I have taken off from work recently."

I think it was then that Bobby realized how much of my life had been put on hold as we worked toward clearing Bobby from the murder charge.

"Fair enough," Bobby said, adding "I will call you in a week or two and we will make plans for when and where you will join us. Believe me, I will never forget that you were there for me when I needed you the most. I promise to always be there for you as well"

The smile was not leaving Bobby's face and his enthusiasm was again contagious. We both seemed to feel the emotions bubbling up toward the surface and in an attempt to quell the potential awkwardness of the moment, we extended our hands toward each other but this time instead of a hug, we both repositioned and resorted to our traditional knuckle bump.

Elaine stood in the distance as if to let us have our time to talk. I caught her smiling at us as Bobby continued with his plan.

I told him to call me when they knew where they would be. Bobby laughed and said, "I am not going to call to tell you where we are, I am going to call to tell you there is a limo on its way to your house. That limo will take you to the private jet which will in turn deliver you, and anyone else you would like to bring along, to where we are."

"You can stay forever if you want to. Anything you wish for will be yours for the asking."

I smiled at him and said "Remember, money can't buy love."

With that, Bobby turned and walked back toward the Dodge Challenger as Elaine sat down in the passenger seat. Bobby drove away and I heard him chirp the tires as he shifted into second gear and I knew my friend was genuinely happy.

Inside the car, as they drove away Bobby said to Elaine, "This car feels strangely familiar. I wonder…" and with that, he reached up to flip down the rear view mirror and there it was, written across the top, 'Bobby + Penny 4 ever'.

He turned toward and Elaine to thank her, "I can't believe you found the exact car I owned all those years ago!"

"It's amazing sometimes how the universe has a way of working these things out. I found it at a dealership in Philadelphia." Elaine said with a smile, "I am glad to be able to reunite you with the memories of your first true love."

Chapter Sixteen

Nearly two weeks passed before I heard from Bobby again. He called me one day while I was still at work. He was using a satellite phone and was calling from some obscure island off the coast of South America. The first thing he did was apologize for having taken so long to call, explaining, "Did you know it takes the fucking lottery people fifteen days to put money into a bank account?" which left them on what he now considered a very tight budget of $10,000 a week as they waited.

I knew he was half joking. With the money he had won with that ticket, he and Elaine could spend $10,000 a week for twenty years and never run out of money.

We laughed as we talked for a while until Bobby's mood turned serious.

He confided in me that he needed to tell me something but had to have my word that I would never tell anyone else what he was about to say.

"It goes without saying that my absolute discretion is promised to you. Tell me anything." I said as I wondered to myself what Bobby could possibly have to tell me.

I heard Bobby take a deep breath as he considered how to start his story.

"Yesterday, Elaine and I were on the beach together enjoying our vacation. It truly is paradise here, Denny. It is perfect. Anyway, we were on the beach when Elaine decided to walk down to the water to get her feet wet. When she turned around, I was talking to a young, and I admit extremely attractive, young woman that was walking on the beach. She had asked for help in finding her hotel that she was certain was close by but was unable to discern from the other hotels along the beach. As it turned out, she was staying at the same resort we had been staying at since we arrived and I pointed out to her which one it was. We exchanged small talk and she laughed at something I said just as Elaine was walking up behind me. The girl casually said "I'll see you at the hotel," as she walked away. I turned toward Elaine who was by now only a couple feet away from me. There was a look in her eyes somewhat reminiscent of that night we saw her pull Katie's hair. To be honest, it startled me for a moment and I asked her what was the matter.

Almost as if she was reprimanding me, she blurted out "Don't you get any ideas."

I started to explain to her that the girl had stopped to ask for directions to her hotel and that as it turned out, we were all staying at the same place. Before I could finish, Elaine cut me off with something that changes things forever. She started by repeating herself, "Don't you get any ideas about any other women or I'll do to you what I did to your wife!"

She was almost smiling as she said it, so for a moment I thought that she was joking with me. I smiled at her and said 'Whatever'. She then looked at me and said. 'I am not joking, Bobby. I am dead serious. I killed Dana and I set that little bitch Katie up for the murder. When you won the lottery the same night that I put my plan into motion it just about fucked everything up.'

I was still in total disbelief as she explained how she had saved the blonde hair from that night at the dealership and how she had taken the lottery ticket with the lipstick print on it and used them to plant evidence. She further explained that she had gone into The Lottery Club program and deleted Katie's name from my 'precious program,' as she called it. Then she said 'Then all that hype with the lottery win almost ruined that.' But I couldn't figure out how she had gotten into the program to begin with and when I said that there was no way she could have figured out my password she said with an almost maniacal grin, "Oh really? How about this... 'I know what you're thinking....and I can prove it?'"

My knees became weak and there was a lump in my throat. Even if I had known what to say, I couldn't speak. She added, 'That's right. *Bigdipper*. Do you really think that you are the ONLY one that can get someone to do anything for you? Let's face it, none of this would have been possible without Denny's help. One night he gave me the password in an effort to prove his love, devotion, and trust in me. I even made it seem like it was his idea. It was really almost too easy. Until winning the lottery nearly destroyed everything.'"

I, too, was in shock. I immediately regretted everything I had ever told Elaine in confidence. I asked Bobby if he was absolutely sure she was telling the truth. Bobby assured me that he was one hundred percent positive.

"And now, because of what she has done, an innocent woman is in prison for life. And because of what I have done, Elaine is free and has $105 million in her bank account."

Bobby admitted that the things she had said had made him more than a little afraid. He insisted that it was plan to play along as though he was okay with it, but he planned to find a way to get Elaine back to the United States where he would inform the authorities of the real truth.

Bobby and I ended the conversation and as I put my phone down, I felt a jolt of fear run up my spine. I was afraid that maybe this time; he really didn't have it covered.

The End.......Not A Chance!

For interesting insight, to email the authors with questions, to post comments, or to learn more about future works by the authors, visit

www.TheLotteryClub.net

The Lottery Club does not end here.

Visit our website for updates on the upcoming sequels of The Club Trilogy

33247692R00110

Made in the USA
Charleston, SC
08 September 2014